SAND DUNES
Dubai Puzha

Krishnadas who is Journalist, Writer and Publisher was Born at Engandiyoor, Trichur, Kerala. Left to UAE in the early seventies. Was a staff of *Reuters Bulletin*, the first English newspaper in UAE, based in Sharjah. Later joined in the *Hongkong Bank* worked until 1998 and returned to India. In UAE he was social worker of Indian Community and participated in literary and social activities. Served as a Journalist, wrote columns regularly for newspapers and magazines about Middle east. During the Gulf war he worked as a reporter to *Desabhmani*. In addition to *Dubaipuzha*, memoirs he wrote a novel *Katalirampangal* (Rumbling seas). His other works are *Marubhoomiyile jalakangal* (The windows of the desert) and *Iruttil Urangathirikkunnu.* (Be awaken in the darkness). Now active in publishing.

Dubai Puzha

When Seagulls Fly Over Dubai Creek

Memoirs

Krishnadas

Translated from Malayalam by
Prabha R. Chatterji

SAND DUNES

SAND DUNES
Kerala, India

SAND DUNES is an imprint of the Green Books

 Green Books
India

www.greenbooksindia.com

Illustrations Courtesy : N.P. Chandrasekharan, Calicut (Kerala)

ISBN : 978 93 88830 71 3

First Impression August 2019

Printed in India by Manipal Technologies Ltd, Manipal

Dubai Puzha
When Seagulls Fly Over Dubai Creek

My son sits at the edge of my bed
and asks me to recite a poem,
A tear falls from my eyes onto the pillow.
My son picks it up, astonished, saying:
'But this is a tear, father, not a poem!'
And I tell him:
'When you grow up, my son,
and read the diwan of Arabic poetry
you'll discover that the word and the tear are twins
and the Arabic poem
is no more than a tear wept by writing fingers

(Nizar Qabbani: A Lesson in Drawing)

Translator's foreword

No man can live this life and emerge unchanged. He will carry forever , however faint, the imprint of the desert, the brand which marks the nomad and he will have within him the yearning to return, weak or insistent according to his nature. This cruel land can cast a spell which no temperate climate can match

(Wilfred Thesiger: Arabian Sands)

During the sixties, countries in the Persian gulf experienced an influx of migrant laborers because of the oil boom. Men came from far and wide; from nearby east African coastal countries of Somalia and Ethiopia as well as far flung Indian subcontinent. The single largest ethnic group in the migrant population consisted of Keralites (also referred to as Malayalis because they speak Malayalam), hailing from the lush green southern state of Indian Union. Because, Kerala was reeling under acute

unemployment when gulf countries
threw open their doors for skilled and unskilled
migrants alike. Still it remains indeed an irony
that men from the land of copious monsoon found
the barren desert extremely fertile to
sow and grow their dreams. Equally glaring was
the irony of Keralites steeped in socialistic
ideologies migrating to hereditary monarchies
in search of livelihood and their remittance boosting
up the economy of Kerala. In any case, the fact
remains that they dared to cross the Arabian sea in
unseaworthy cargo ships, many drowned as boats
capsized. Of those who perished in the sea there are
no records, no names, no count. Those who reached
the shores didn't
have an easy life either. Many started off as
unskilled laborers and slowly and steadily built
up their lives. They literally wilted in the
scorching desert to prosper in life. Life was
harsh and cruel, but they had hope.

That was only one side of the story. On the
other side, in Kerala the label "*Gulfukaran*"
became an identity and earned respectability.

No one bothered about the nitty-gritty of their job description. Besides, the label was so dazzling that it blinded the near and dear ones and far away bystanders to the travails and tribulations the Gulfukaran suffered to save and sent money home. With the result that thousands more took the same path. Keralites can easily assimilate the ethos and pathos of the situation. Some prospered, for others the struggle never ended. Today despite all odds and ironies, the Malayali diaspora in the Gulf stands at 2.5 million with majority of them being there for decades either by choice or by compulsion. Nevertheless each Gulf Malayali's ultimate dream is to retire to his own little green patch in Kerala.

Walking down the memory lane spanning three decades of stay, Krishnadas presents a collage of real, ordinary people who find themselves in not so ordinary circumstances in the Gulf countries. Events such as the dissolution of Trucial States, communist upheaval in Yemen, the formation of UAE.

the Iran-Iraq war, the urbanization of UAE suburbs, Iraq's highhandedness on Kuwait, the dissolution of Soviet Union, the Palestine conflict etc.- become not geopolitical markers of time but changemakers which influence the social fabric of migrants. Nostalgia for homeland runs as a strong undercurrent throughout the narration; also submerged tensions surface at several places. Imagination and experience add an extra dimension to the sketches of people and places. Extracts from the pre-Islamic and post modern Arabic poems open a window to peep into the Arabian culture- a way of life as it was and as it is.

Dubai Puzha reflects the struggles of migrants to accommodate themselves in alien soil. Though Krishnadas focuses on the Malayali diaspora, the theme has universal relevance. I have taken care to ensure that nothing is lost in translation. In rendering the Arabic poems into English, access to the following proved helpful: *An Anthology of Modern Arabic Poems*

compiled by Khouri and Algar (University of
California Press, 1974); *The Gateway to Modern
Arabic Poetry* by Mezyed and Al Assadi (Published
by Art-Gate Associations, Romania 2007),
Arabian Poetry for English Readers by W.A.
Coulston (1881); The Golden Odes or Seven Poems
suspended in the Temple of Mecca
(English translation *of al-sab-al Muallaqt* by
F.E Johnson(1893), The Rubaiyat of
Omar Khayyam by Edward Fitzgerald(1859)
and other web versions.

Prabha R. Chatterji

Contents

Prologue
DUBAI PUZHA

I wish I could wade through you to reach the moon,
I hear pebbles rattle at the bottom,
And sparrows in thousands twitter on the trees
Are you a river or a forest of tears?

(Badr Shakir Al Sayyab: The River and the Death-)

Often, overwhelmed by a sense of alienation I would seek solace on the shores of *Dubai Puzha* . To me, she had all the charm and beauty of the silvery streams of my village, thousands of miles away. Compelling circumstances had uprooted me at a very young age, from my lush green village and transplanted in a dry, desert city. Unaccustomed to the land and its people I would stand on the shore gazing at the channel of blue water glistening in the morning sun and would feel strangely comforted. I would absorb the multiple sounds and sights, the rhythmic dynamics of life that

17

filled the surroundings; I would be reminded of the ancient civilizations that evolved on riverbanks. And I would feel optimistic and confident.

I still cherish those images. The river like a blue band; dhows, big and small rollicking in the river ; dilapidated houses with old fashioned wind towers on rooftops and their dancing reflections on water; narrow lanes and alleys filled with the scent of heritage; old men on the doorsteps enjoying their hookah and chatting in Persian or Arabic; sea gulls flapping their wings flying off from the water surface reminiscent of a Van Gogh painting..........

*Dubai puzha, Dubai river? There isn't anything like that-*many summarily dismissed my imagery. A few others were a little more accommodative: *Oh! You mean the creek?* Well, it is all a matter of opinion, isn't it?. A narrow channel of seawater flowing inland- indeed it is a creek, the Dubai creek . But to my homesick mind it was a *river* and will ever remain so. *Dubai Puzha* brought back the riotous colors of my childhood and rejuvenated me. Though the shores were brown and barren, the waves echoed the sweet melodies of the mangrove forests, I was certain....

The creek cleaved Dubai city into two- *Deira* and *Bur Dubai* and then flowed further inland beyond the automatic bridges and finally disappeared in the sand bed. The bridges were too far away from the city centre and hence water taxis called *abhras* linked Deira and Bur Dubai. These motorized boats were navigated by boisterous Iranian youths with stained teeth and a mop of unruly hair. *Abhras* were always crowded; in each trip they transported hundreds of passengers each way. Their synchronized orbits presented a pulsating picture of Dubai city.

There used to be a dredger permanently stationed in the Dubai creek. It continually scooped out silt and sediment from the depths and made the creek navigable for huge freighters. When giant cargo ships rolled in blowing loud horns, automatic bridges opened and water surged towards the shores.

But the glamour of the creek was the fleet of hundreds of dhows anchored on both sides stretched over a kilometer or more. Their strange sails and stranger crew filled onlookers with curiosity and excitement. A cacophony of languages - Swahili, Somali, Persian, Urdu, Malayalam- floated in the air.

I was told: *from time immemorial dhows are the life lines of Dubai. Sans Dhows, Dubai is soulless...*

That was indeed true. The market streets of Dubai came alive because of the dhows. They carried dates and tea to east African port cities of Mozambique, Mogadishu and Zanzibar; gold bars to the inscrutable shores of Indian peninsula; electronic goods and automobiles to the Iranian port cities of Bandar Abbas and Siraf. In exchange they brought back perfumes from Africa, spices from India and sheep from Iran. Dhows, *abhras*, and sea gulls together with an exuberance of lights and shades , drew a thousand formless designs on the water surface; the waves dissipated accompanying sounds. Oblivious of all this bustle, the blue water flowed into the sea.

It was three decades ago that three of us, cousins, reached those alien shores with the dream of making it big in life. A kindred soul arranged a temporary shelter for us- a small mud plastered Arab hut with a tiny ventilator. We were worn out and sick after weeks of harrowing voyage across the Arabian sea. During the first few days we just ate and slept , woke up to eat

21

and slept again. We didn't dare to stir out. *Alien land, alien people, even the dwellings looked alien.* The long robes and guttural language of the people terrified us. Outside our shelter there were clusters of thatched huts. We could see women with black cloth over their faces. An Arab gentle man often came over and knocked at our door. If we delayed in responding, he would plaintively shout *ya Allah, ya Allah.* Whatever he hissed through his clenched golden teeth, we were at a loss to understand and that scared us even more. Later we came to know : that he was our landlord; that he was cautioning us not to waste water and electricity; that local people often spoke both Parsi and Arabic ; that the head scarf is *Keffiyeh* and the braided rope that kept it in place is *agal*; that the black robe women wore is *naqab*…

After several days of rest we began venturing out in the evenings to experience the sights and sounds of the city. Some Arab men smiled at us seductively , others stopped their cars and offered to take us home. Very carefully we steered clear of them all. We had been forewarned - : *alien city, alien ways*…

Dubai Puzha

The path that snaked among the jumble of huts took us to the waterfront. Mundane sights greeted us there- donkey carts loaded with huge barrels marked British Petroleum; standing next to them were Arab merchants shouting *gas gas;* women selling sardines and snacks. From the waterfront a short straight road stretched to the thronging market place- the *souk.* My mind has retained colorful murals of the rural scene. A middle-aged woman with bunches of tobacco- *naqab* tightly clinging to her face revealing just a pair of kohl-lined wide eyes; over there an old man with a spread of dried lemons in aluminum trays supported on a wooden crate; the gurgling sound as he draws on his hookah. Elsewhere an old woman smearing batter thinly in a saucepan propped on top of a kerosene stove. The thin layer instantly drying up into brown crunchy wafer. Next to it a counter displaying boiled *chickpeas* garnished with chopped onions and lemon. And then the vegetable vendor with fresh bunches of spinach, leeks, celery and mint. A sprightly lad selling *suleimani tea,* moving briskly among the crowd with small cups immersed in a bucketful of water. The aroma of *Suleimani* spiced with cardamom and cloves filling the air...

Dubai of the past had none of the glamour or grandiose of today. But the life that went on along those shores presented a picture of vigor and vitality.

Trade and Customs Office was on the shores of Bur Dubai. A few paces away stood the offices of Sheikh Maktoum, the *majlis* and the Royal Palace. *Majlis* was the council house where the sheikhs met and drew the road map for the development and progress of the nation. About a century ago, Dubai had a thriving business in pearls. Dubai pearls had high demand in world market. Iranians crossed over to Dubai to dive for pearls. Close on their heels came Hindu and Khwaja merchants. They bargained hard and pleased with the deals sailed back to Bombay (now *Mumbai*). Around that time Sindhi merchants began settling down in Dubai. But with the depression in the thirties , Dubai pearl market too crashed. Silence descended on the shores of Dubai. Consumer needs of a nation couldn't be met with just camel milk and dates or figs. People died of starvation, so say the history books. Later global economy recovered, but not the pearl business because by then cultured pearls had entered the market. However Dubai got a new lease of life as a busy commercial hub, a trading port. Those muscular men who dived for delicate pearls became porters loading and unloading cargo at the port and warehouses. In the fifties British company Gray Mackenzie arrived on the shores to control the water ways followed by the British Bank (today's Hong Kong Shanghai Bank) to manage the finances related to customs and trade. *Indian Rupee* became the gulf currency. These are all old stories, but important subplots in the saga of an empire where the sun never set. The older generation of Arabs still prefer to deal in *Indian Rupee* .

In front of the customs office stood rows and rows of warehouses. I befriended Bashir a Keralite. He was a customs clerk, and he became my guide. *To be employable*, Bashir said, *one must acquire a skill and that demands hard work*. And so I began as his assistant. I remember those sizzling summer days spent in the warehouses- identifying the crates by matching the logos and labels in the Bill of Lading. I made an earnest and sincere attempt to be adept at this job so that eventually I can stand on my legs. Thousands of crates- strewn around haphazardly ... inside and outside the warehouses; *turn them around, find the identification marks, match them, count them , tally the count*...... Harsh work and harsher surroundings. All for a better life, I consoled myself, so that I could soon proudly write home *yes, I have got a job now*....... But my struggle continued with no respite. Debts mounted and so did despair and frustration. My sweat and tears fell on the hot sand and evaporated instantly, as if the desert was thirsty for more.

Later we shifted to the Chettuva Lodge in the *Sikat Al Har* street. It was a huge house with six or seven rooms and in each room several rows of bunk beds. There I unexpectedly ran into Abdullakkutty. He was rolling out *parathas* for dinner, with a rickety rusted table fan to ward off the scorching heat. I was taken aback. Years ago, fed up with rolling *beedies* in our village market he had boarded a train bound for Bombay to try his luck there. We had wished him well then. But luck had catapulted him from Mumbai to Dubai and transformed him into a cook at the Chettuva Lodge. He was excited to see me and gave me a hearty smile. He had so much to share. He pulled out a stack of Malayalam newspapers. *Didn't you know about the Naxalite activities in Kerala ? Pulpalli, Nagaur, K. Venu, Ajitha*....... ?

Abdullakkutty went on nonstop. All that he said was indeed news to me; nothing less than a thriller. For months I hadn't read anything in Malayalam; a sense of loss slowly permeated through me- would I have forgotten the script?. I leafed through one of the magazines lying next to me. The serial I used to read once upon a time hadn't concluded yet......

Those days *Sikat Al Her* was the red light area of Dubai. Brisk business went on all the time. In the evenings the terrace of the lodge became our vantage point to enjoy the scenes below with the accompaniment of scents and sounds that wafted up. Some men hurried through the street with obvious disgust, others bargained patiently at each door.

Kam ? (how much)

Ashrin (20)

la Ashra? (how about ten?)

ya Allah, ya Allah

The women were from Pakistan, Iran Egypt and Palestine......some with painted faces and a few others with naqabs... They stood at their door and solicited customers. *Hijras* kept them company with music and dance. Tea and snack vendors made quick business too. Many a time loud rejoicings turned into ribaldry......

Later in search of greener pastures I relocated to other emirates. Still *Dubai Puzha* beckoned me and I visited her often. Strolling along the lively waterfront, enjoying a cruise in the *abhra*, watching the swaying dhows..... But the neighborhood I knew so well had changed beyond recognition. The tiny Arab hut where we took refuge during the initial days , those clusters of thatched huts, those narrow lanes and alleys ....all had disappeared, demolished to be precise. As it yielded the space to a huge, expansive dry dock. The past has become a memorable collage ...

I remember the time when Iraq got embroiled with Iran over the control of the narrow *Shatt-al-Arab* waterway on the Iran-Iraq border. A War that went on for eight turbulent years. Millions died. The Arab block including Dubai stood firm with Iraq and Saddam. But majority of Dubaites shared ancestral and heritage links with Iranians. For them the war was an ideological and emotional dilemma. Ibrahim, my Arab colleague, praised Khomeini, denounced Saddam and hissed curses at the sheikhs.

Iran threatened to block the strategic *Hormuz strait*. American warships prowled in the gulf waters waiting to pounce. Traders didn't want to get caught in the crossfire and risk lives and goods, hence trade came to a standstill and dhows remained anchored on the shores. Electronic goods and automobiles intended for Iran lay heaped up in Dubai warehouses. With the dhows grounded, the crew, bored and listless looked for ways and means to kill time. Some just slept in the dhows or loitered on the shore ; a few queer ones spent time indulging young boys. When the war finally got over there was a sigh of relief all around. Trade picked up, the shores of Dubai became active again.

Memoirs of Dubai is incomplete without Josephettan, my *Guru*. A staunch communist and an excellent orator, he would seize any and every opportunity to extol the virtues of socialism. He would thunder: *Fortune seekers from all over the globe flock to the Arab countries. But among them can you spot a single person from the socialist block ?*

Those were the eighties. Josephettan believed and made others believe in the infallibility and unassailability of the socialist block. Then, in the nineties Eastern Europe and Soviet Union disintegrated. For several of us it was a personal tragedy and we lost sleep for many days. I was sure Josephettan must have been shattered too. By that time he had returned to Kerala. And then, contrary to his belief, planeloads of Russians descended on Dubai, lured by the Arab riches. Out of their suitcases came Russian watches, telescopes, cameras and the like which they spread on the shores of Dubai. Revolution was over, now they were street vendors and hawkers. Their women , dressed up in their finery, looked for customers in Dubai hotels and busy shopping malls.

Josephettan had to leave Dubai under duress because his business had run into bad weather. He owned a small 'Clothing & Tailoring Shop' in Dubai. Mounting debts led him almost to the doorsteps of jail. Those who knew him denounced him: "Well, he brought it on himself ". Their fingers were raised at his ineptitude, irresponsibility, lack of business sense,

above all his politics….... Finally he managed to escape. Under the cover of darkness, he climbed onto a dhow bound for the coast of Gujarat and from there somehow reached his village in Kerala.

For me, life eventually changed for the better. In the new job I was caught up in a whirlwind of never ending trainings. Management courses, novel marketing strategies, digitization , plastic money…… Trainings were held on the shores of Dubai, in a skyscraper- the new headquarters of the hundred year old Bank which had arrived in Dubai during colonial days to conduct trade with Indian peninsula. Through the plate glass windows of the new building I could see the Dubai *Puzha* below, picture perfect. Each training concluded with the usual formalities followed by a gala dinner at the penthouse. Whenever boredom crept in, I turned to the *Puzha* for company. At night she provided a kaleidoscopic view of the luminous city. Dhows with red beacon and loud siren, abhras with the swinging hurricane lamps, … I would drift into old memories...

Wind towers on roof tops, clay and coral huts, houses with doors and windows opening to the creek, the old customs and warehouse with crates scattered all around….. Relics of the past have been erased , yet heart searches….

Bygone days! Those painted and veiled sex workers of S*ikkat al her* street disappeared long ago. Even earlier than that, camels and caravans confined themselves to the pages of Arabian folktales. Time sets in motion a continuous process of transformation of landscapes and people. Culture and traditions are being reinterpreted. Like the camel. New generation feeds it cola, prepares the poor animal for the camel race to win handsome monetary rewards…. The dhows and *abhras* add on to the tourist attractions during the annual international shopping festivals…. Dubai is flourishing and flashing its wealth. The city's splendor reflects in the Dubai puzha and like a bejeweled beauty she flows.

Decades later when it was time to say goodbye to the Persian gulf, I didn't feel any pain. Even so, the special bond with *Dubai Puzha* remains; my nostalgic sighs might be ruffling her surface at times, I am certain… ∎

THE CROSSING

One
The Hajar Mountains

Rocky, precipitous Hajar mountains. Starting from Hormuz strait it stretches southeast hugging the coast of Arabian peninsula. Several peaks proudly rise to a height of 2000 feet or more. An accumulation of dry, barren limestone boulders, interspersed very rarely with dreamlike valleys.

Like the steep highs and lows of tumultuous youth - he thought when he sighted Hajar ranges for the first time. Personally he too was passing through a similar turbulent, uncertain phase. He was crossing the unknown seas to reach an unknown promised land. Not that he was alone, there were several other passengers nursing similar dreams. The cargo boat that sailed between the Malabar coast and the Persian Gulf was not equipped to carry passengers. Tormented by hunger and thirst, weary to the core by dizziness, nausea and weak stomach the human cargo was in a miserable state. They fervently dreamt of reaching the shores. Days became weeks, but the journey seemed to be never ending, land could not be sighted. They were lost in the vast ocean, rudderless at sea. As the vessel plunged into troughs and climbed onto crests, huge sharks surfaced. Flying fish demonstrated their acrobatics, wild and strange creatures roared, poisonous water snakes floated around the boat. It was like a safari through a marine zoo.

During that journey he became aware of many facets of the deep and boundless ocean

> Turbulent yet placid, hostile yet benign
> The sea embraced the horizon
> Her mysterious depths, blue and dark
> Brimmed with creatures wild and strange

That journey also taught him what it was to be poor, to be hungry, to be thirsty. He learned that the transition from wretchedness to greed to evil, is smooth and at times quick , because the dividing lines are thin. He understood the desperation of helpless men caught in the claws of death, because he was one among them. Loud prayers and placations to gods and prophets alike ruptured the air. The fierce choppy Arabian sea was so unlike the serene beauty he had so often enjoyed from the safety of the coast. Much later he would write to his friends that the vast ocean was as formidable as a dense forest-

Losing all hopes they had resigned themselves to a watery grave and then like a revelation they saw the blue cliffs of the Hajar mountains and then slowly the panoramic view of the entire range was unraveled for them.

Jutting out into the sea, the cliffs rose up into the sky and cast reflections on the water below. Only when the boat got closer did they realize that the mountain was mostly dry and lifeless. But still, it kindled hopes for a better tomorrow, for a new beginning. It was winter; sun shone feebly and briefly over the ranges and then sank into the horizon leaving a golden glow over the cliffs. Finally darkness descended and enveloped the earth. From the boat they could see a few specks of light scattered in the mountains. To them those were messages of compassion and love from an unknown land.

They sailed for one more day hugging the coastline and finally anchored at the base of the foothills of Hajar. Steep hills rose up in front of them blocking their way. They were stupefied. Life was presenting itself in the most formidable and challenging form. They broke into small groups and began climbing over the boulders, brushing aside prickly thorns and thistles. Parched throat and worn out legs forced them to rest frequently on the rocks . It seemed to be a never ending journey. As time dragged on thirst, hunger and despair assailed them more and more.

It was November. Sun had set, in some corner of the cloudy sky moon was hesitantly making an appearance. They could feel cold slowly building up. Wild animals howled and roared somewhere in the mountains.

Bewildered and frantic they continued their journey- descending somewhere, ascending elsewhere. At every turn more cliffs blocked their way. It grew dark and cold. They were trapped in the labyrinthine mountain ranges, clueless which way to proceed. And then at some point instinct took over. They capped their ears and listened for familiar sounds. They could hear- somewhere, far away feeble sounds of vehicles. Climbing over rocks and squeezing in between clefts, the weary travelers dragged themselves and headed towards the sounds. As they got closer sounds became clearer. Sounds of vehicles and voices of men- what a relief!. Headlights of the vehicles had lit up the vault of the sky. They moved forward.

They had reached the tiny township of Khor Fakkan, a rather nondescript medieval town with rough narrow gravel roads and old obsolete buildings. Donkeys brayed in what seemed to be the main avenue.. Women clad in black burqa moved around hastily and chatting loudly. Automobiles struggled through the rough pebble-strewn roads. Perhaps there wasn't a single vehicle in Khor Fakkan which had ever known the feel of a satin smooth road, he thought. The town was slowly waking up from the exhaustion of dawn to dusk fasting and getting ready for the ritual *ifthar* feasting.

Limping, the exhausted travelers hauled themselves forward. The locals greeted them: *Salaam alaikam.*

Aroma of delicious food filled the air and they entered an eatery. Hunger had stripped them off their urbane niceties and reduced them to the status of cavemen. Gurgling down large quantities of water they hunched over and gorged on whatever food was set before them.

Khor Fakkan- a tiny coastal town nestling in the lap of the blue Hajar mountains. Its market street served the needs of nearby hamlets and its tiny port attended to the minimal needs of dhows and ships which passed that way, the lonely lighthouse twinkled and guided the fishermen.

Those days Khor Fakkan and other coastal hamlets were swamped with migrants. Almost everyday boats unloaded people from India, Pakistan, Afghanistan and Iran. Miserable and distraught, these refugees had no other go but to exploit the kindness and compassion of locals, especially during the Ramzan month. Local authorities too took a lenient view.

For him and his companions everything was new and strange. *Alien landscape, alien people, alien language, alien smells.* That night they camped at the base of the foothills . Earth was hard and cold. Their thin shawls could offer no defense against the cold; they couldn't sleep. As night progressed, temperature dipped further. They gathered twigs and lit a fire. In the glow and warmth of the fire they shared their thoughts and dreams for a while and then one by one slowly dozed off. He couldn't sleep. Alone in an unfamiliar terrain thousands of miles away from dear and near ones, he felt miserable. Immature and impetuous, did he make a rash and reckless decision? He felt tormented, skeptical.

Night was foggy. Eerie howls and wild roars floated in the air. Clouds that scattered the moonlight disappeared making way for a clear blue sky with a sprinkle of twinkling stars. And then *prayer call* rose from a nearby mosque announcing the arrival of dawn. Other mosques in the neighborhood soon joined in chorus. Elsewhere roosters too crowed in acknowledgement. Donkeys brayed as Bedouins climbed on and guided them through the streets to begin a new journey.

New Dawn. For them this would be an unforgettable day, first day in a new land. His agonized mind had gradually found peace. Jubilant sounds of a new day, new beginning enveloped him.

Two
A Lost Lamb

He stood against the backdrop of the blue mountain range, anxiously waiting for the sounds of a savior - a vehicle. Sun was about to set, soon it will be dark and cold. With short sleeved cotton shirt, and almost bare feet he was ill equipped to fight the November cold. Unfamiliar terrain plagued him with anguish and uncertainty, the whistling wind was bouncing off from the depths of his heart….. He had lost his way.

He was trying to locate a long lost friend in Khor Fakkan and then he got lost. For the last two days he and his companions were camping at Kalba under a tree. That temporary shelter was the courtesy of Hamsa, a compatriot they had accidentally met. Hamsa, was a cook with the Public Works Department. He was kind enough to provide them with a few utensils, and essential groceries. They had put together stones and twigs and set up a fireplace to cook. In the night they tried to sleep under the tree but cold wouldn't let them. So they gathered more twigs and lit a fire that would last through the night. Nearby stray camels tugging at and champing thorny twigs disturbed the silence of the night. Far away in the rocky hills jackals howled in chorus.

Earlier to that they had walked for one whole night and a full day from Khor Fakkan to reach Kalba. They had begun the trek with great enthusiasm. The mountain path led to Dubai, at least that is what they were told. Initially they enjoyed the desert sights- the blue rocky mountains reaching for the skies; thorny bushes symbolizing the wretchedness of the desert; grazing camels.... But soon the repetitive scenes bored them. Moreover thirst and fatigue distressed them. Overhead, the sun blazed in all its severity. They did sight a river ahead.... Shouts of anticipation and excitement filled the air.....

They walked fast. But the closer they got, farther the river receded...

Mirage!

Till that day they had read about this illusion only in books.....

They walked on wearily, eventually they would have collapsed one by one. But then their ears picked up sounds; the sound of an engine, twittering of birds and rippling of water! The river of life was nearby. Their spirits were revived.

They had reached a farm at the base of the foothills of Kalba. Lush green fields of barley, maize and vegetables stretched before them. Water channels crisscrossed the fields. Flocks of birds flew about chirping merrily. Two Bedouin kids armed with canes supervised the watering.

The weary travelers drank water from the channels to their hearts content, refreshed themselves and rested under the green bushes. That was when they met and befriended Hamsa. His story was not very different from theirs. Two years ago he too had climbed onto a cargo boat that set sail from Bombay and headed for the gulf . In course of time he became a cook. Hamsa was staying nearby in a small tent with his Pakistani employer. He was frank. " I can't accommodate you there. But can provide necessary groceries". That is how they made a temporary shelter in Kalba underneath a tree. Two days later he hitchhiked a ride to Khor Fakkan - in search of a long lost friend. Unfortunately he couldn't locate the friend.

It was getting dark, panic gripped him. He had to get back to Kalba, to his companions who were waiting for him under a tree. He was fervently hoping for the roaring sound of a saviour- a vehicle towards Kalba.

At last he saw a pair of beaming headlights rising up in the horizon and then heard the roar of an engine. A pickup van appeared and stopped right in front of him. An Arab sat at the wheel with his young son next to him. In the trailer a pair of sheep, perhaps a recent purchase from the Khor Fakkan market. Arab gestured to him to get in with the sheep. The vehicle rolled forward and soon they were cruising on a coastal road. Chilly sea breeze forced him to snuggle in between the sheep, but the sheep not interested fidgeted away.

Moon had risen. The sea appeared opalescent as waves broke into gleaming white foam. The blue mountains had transformed into dark sinister titans ready to swallow him. Small wild animals hunting for crabs on the shore ran away frightened and dazzled by the headlight of the pickup van.

He tried to remember the name of the traveler who preferred to live unrecognized in alien territories. Perhaps these unfamiliar roads would lead him to the wonderland of Aladdin. Or perhaps he was already traveling in the mysterious world of Aladdin.....

Finally, the van stopped at a crowded noisy quarter. A middle class Arab neighborhood with well-lit modest houses built close to a wall. His benefactor signaled again- this time to get down from the van. Then he was led inside a house and made to join a group of people seated around large round trays of food; heaps of rice and meat. Hunger got the better of him. It didn't matter to him that all of them were eating from the same plate. *Alien land.. alien customs...*

After the meal, the Arab gentleman talked to him, he stood there like an idiot. He couldn't understand a word except *Hindi, Hindi.* He tried to guess the gist

" Out there you can find your people, Hindi people, go there. Goodbye"

He stared helplessly at the Arab's face and then stepped out into the dark narrow lane. It was deserted. Here? Who? Where? What people? A hostage to his

48

own helplessness and vulnerability, he could do nothing but howl like a mad man.

In the darkness that enveloped him he sensed movements and heard voices. A group of strangers came towards him. When a man with pock marks on his face came forward and took his hand, all he could do was blurt out desparately :

-Are you a Malayali?

-Yes, I am. Come with me, son

That was Satish Chandran from Thiruvanantha-puram. That night he stayed with Chandrettan.

Three
Road to Dubai

Hamsa not only arranged for their travel from Kalba to Dubai. But also paid for it.

The jeep arrived in the evening. There were other passengers too, newbies like them. The driver was a Baluchi, and with him in the front sat *Hajiar* **(1)** who wore a huge turban. Hajiar, kind and compassionate, had taken it upon himself to transport new migrants to their desired destination.

Their jeep jumped and rolled over the hilly terrain, clambered up steep ascends and hurtled down equally steep descends. Weeks of starvation and nausea while at sea, followed by days of irregular feasting on land had terribly upset the metabolic cycle of the passengers and most of them were suffering from flatulence. When the rough, uneven mountain road shook and tossed the jeep and the passengers incessantly, odor most foul filled the air.. Baluchi driver protested- *Pals! I need fresh air.*

Baluchi would stop the jeep, get out and inhale deeply. So did the passengers. The cool and misty mountain air refreshed them. He looked around- an unfamiliar land with dark mountains. Up above in the vault of the sky , moon and a few stars. He felt nostalgic- was it the same moon that peeped through the foliage into the courtyard of his village home? His companions seemed happy and hopeful. Would all their dreams come true soon ?

They reached Sharjah very late in the night. Streetlights had lit up the city. Inside the Trucial Oman Scouts campus, the communication towers stood tall and sinister with red lights at the top. Hajiar led them to the courtyard of a mosque. Then in very kind tones he said *"Children, don't worry about anything. Stay here. I will come and call you when it is time to leave."*

It was a magnificent marble courtyard adorned with huge chandeliers. The electric lamps seemed to radiate messages of benevolence. The wayfarers stretched their weary legs on the marble floors and were soon asleep. When *azan* call for the early morning prayer resounded through the air, Hajiar came to gather them. As they walked to the jeep Hajiar said *"This is Ramzan time. You won't get any food during day time. So let us first eat something and then proceed"*. They entered a nearby eatery. Hajiar paid for the khima curry and paratha they ate.

When they finally got into the taxi headed for Dubai, Hajiar blessed them and said goodbye. *"All the Best, children"*. Did Haji's words leave him misty eyed, he can't remember .

Today, after so many years, when he looks back, gratitude overwhelms him. Life took him through many a cryptic twists and turns. But at each critical intersection strangers appeared extending a helping hand. Hamsa, Chandrettan, Hajiar and several more….. the names are indelible.

Morning.

They were on their way to Dubai.

Sun's rays filtered through the fog. FM Music filled the vehicle. A smooth straight road lay ahead. Leaving behind the streetlights of Sharjah's main avenue, their jeep raced forward. Oblivious of the fact that he had lost his footwear somewhere en route, he dozed off lulled by the cool breeze. ■

Stay! Let us weep, while memory tries to trace
The long-lost fair one's sand-girt dwelling-place;
Though the rude winds have swept the sandy plain,
Still some faint traces of that spot remain.
My comrades reined their coursers by my side,
And "Yield not-yield not to despair" they cried
Tears were my sole reply, yet what avail
Tears shed on sands, or sighns upon the gale?

(Imrul Qais-: The Golden Odes (2))

SHELTERS OF SHARJAH

One
Rolla is my witness

Majestically spreading its leafy branches and hanging roots, Rolla, the banyan tree stood on the main avenue, in the heart of Sharjah city. It provided shade and shelter to weary travelers; thousands of birds flocked to its branches and set up their nests. Homeless laborers and nomadic traders had implicit trust in Rolla. They left their tin boxes which contained their entire, meager savings on the branches or forks of Rolla. It was indeed an unusual and curious sight. During summer months someone would leave a huge mud pot filled with water and a glass under the tree. Taxis waited for passengers under its shade and drivers would shout *Ajmaan, Dubai*.... From the primary school nearby, children's voices radiated and rustled Rolla's leaves. During Ramzaan and Haj days Rolla would be adorned with colorful lights.

The tree was a reference point in the daily lives of Sharjah residents- locals and migrants alike. New friendships were forged and old ones reinforced under the Rolla. *"Ok, then let's meet tomorrow at Rolla"*, that was how we said goodbye. Seated under the Rolla we shared homeland news, discussed literature and politics.

The bark and branches of Rolla had by then begun to wither away, an obvious proof of its advanced age. But nobody knew how old it was. The older generation remembered the tree as part of their childhood. Was it there during the riotous days of Wahabi movement ? What about the time when Arabian shores were known as the Pirate Coast in the sailor's maps? Did it witness the frantic efforts of the East India Company to take possession of the Persian Gulf? Nobody was sure. But one thing was certain. In 1930, when colonial government began setting up Sharjah as their air force base to fly to India, Rolla was present.

We, a bunch of desperate young men in search of jobs hung around Rolla round the clock- morning, noon, evening, night… Rolla witnessed our hopeful trips to Dubai and Ajman and our disappointed returns. Glowing with hope in the twilight and shedding tears of dew in the wee hours, she empathized with us. When frustration drove some of us to join a construction company in Ajman as daily wage workers; when we worked overnight shifts bending and bunching iron rods to size with Suleimani tea to keep us awake; when disgusted with such a life Ravindran cut his wrist; when authorities promptly locked him up in jail for attempted suicide- all along Rolla sheltered and comforted us under her canopy.

Finally old age took its toll. Bereft of leaves, the trunk stood brown and barren, reduced to a skeleton, like a forgotten piece of history. And then one fine day the city authorities came and removed it. But Rolla is forever etched in our memory because she was the sole witness of our aspirations and agonies.

Modern Sharjah has a brand new, absolutely modern Rolla Square, complete with a digital picture of Rolla at the centre.

Two

Colonial Masquerades

A coy, charming village belle. That was Sharjah decades ago. Not flashy, not flamboyant, and certainly not fashionable.

Narrow lanes, old streets, fragrance of oil lamps and perfumes, breakers frothing at the coast, starlit blue sky. A tiny little Arab heritage town.

As early as 1853 Britain had strategically bound several of the sheikhdoms of the Pirate Coast with a Perpetual Maritime Truce and that was the genesis of the Trucial States. In 1930s, Sharjah became the air base from where the imperial aircrafts took off for India and other eastern colonies. While other members of the Trucial Coast Alliance turned to trade and pearl business to augment their revenue, Sheikh of Sharjah leased out the town to the Royal Air Force and lived on the annual rent. British Royal Air Force kept the town awake day and night. Army vehicles growled through the streets nonstop. During the late sixties, when the communist movement shook southern

Arabia (Yemen today) the British had to evacuate Aden and subsequently the colonial forces were concentrated in Sharjah.

The main avenue of the city lay stretched to the coast with the oil depots of the British Petroleum conveniently located alongside. On the wharfs and piers that jutted out to the sea, British soldiers could be seen fishing and listening to music that flowed from their transistors. Army men roamed around in the town, alone and in groups. Their shouts and sounds filled the neighborhood.

Leaving Dubai, I had taken refuge in Sharjah. Those days there were two military camps in Sharjah - The Royal Air Force and the Trucial Oman Scouts. Trucial Oman Scouts later became the UAE Defense Force.

Sridharettan and Ismail worked for the Trucial Oman Scouts. Sridharettan was a clerk, a fat, flabby man with a mole on his face. Once, for a minor lapse in duty, he was made to run ten rounds in the parade ground with typewriter on his head. Later, when anyone alluded to that incident, a shadow of despair would darken his face. Ismail was a steward in the Officers' Mess. "Going home" was an annual ritual for Ismail. Preparatory to this event, he would begin stuffing his old fashioned trunk with everything foreign- clothes, perfumes, gadgets.......We would sit around watching him pack. He would board the ship *Dumas*. It took him six or seven days to reach the port of Bombay, from there another three or four days by train to his village in Kerala. Ismail would return with loads of homemade snacks wrapped in local newspaper. We would relish the snacks, then spread out the oil smeared wrappers and eagerly read homeland news. Another inmate of the lodge was Ramunni uncle, an elderly gentleman who owned a handicrafts emporium which catered to mainly Western customers. He returned from work very late at night or at times not at all. Naturally rumors did the rounds - that he had many affairs, even with Arab women ....

A sprawling white mansion stood on a rather isolated spot on the main avenue that extended to the Royal Air Force campus. Built in old Yemeni style, the mansion had the look and feel of a haunted house. It was large enough to accommodate several lodges. We stayed in one of the dormitories. The house owner Ahmed Saleh and his family occupied one part of the building. The Saleh family had fled from Aden, during the communist uprising. Mr Saleh was a wholesale trader in the fish market. Pickup vans and trucks with the unmistakable odor of fish crowded the front yard. Saleh and family spoke Arabic and English with Yemeni accent. Saleh's son Mohammed was a handsome, educated, well informed young man. He was aware of the communist movement in Kerala and its torch bearer EMS. I asked him once why their family had to flee from Yemen. Answer was simple. Ahmed Saleh was a member of the rebel group. Arabs believed in blood for blood and life for life. When communists won, it was pay back time for rebels. Salehs got panicky and fled the scene. Later I would meet several such refugees in various parts of UAE.

Indian migrants- mostly Keralites- lived together as a close-knit community. Almost all of them worked in the British establishments such as offices of Royal Air Force, Trucial Omani Scouts, the *NAAFI* –(Naval, Army and Air Force Institutions) or Malcolm Club. Parameswaran was a barman at the Malcolm Club. His working hours extended beyond midnight. At times he would receive huge tips on such days he would whisper to me *"tomorrow we will go and see a movie"*.

Thus I spent several days, jobless, penniless, at the mercy of others. I saw lots of Hindi movies in an open air theatre nearby. *Love in Tokyo, Milan, Pathar ke Sanam, Farz*.... During winter months mist and fog drenched us and during summer months we sweated profusely. Pakistanis formed good part of the audience. When the Indian flag or Hindu gods appeared on the screen, they would sneer and shout obscenities. Hatred towards Indians and intolerance to Hinduism were the hallmarks of an average Pakistani.

Across the road there were clusters of thatched huts which were a settlement of Sindhi refugees from Pakistan. Parameswaran was interested in a Sindhi girl and would often go and peep into her hut. One day he was caught, given a good thrashing and handed over to the police. The police bet him black and blue, I was sure. With mercy petition in hand, we ran from pillar to post to get him released. Finally we managed to connect with an influential member of a Sheikh family and got him released. Parameswaran came back tamed and tonsured .

Those days even a brief spell of occasional rain would turn the main avenue of Sharjah into a muddy, slushy pit. During summer months Rolla was the centre of the city life. Hindi film songs from the Indian restaurants in the neighborhood filled the air. The Police Station next door had the grandeur of a heritage building. Perhaps it must have been a palace earlier because a huge canon adorned its front yard. Beyond the police station lay a park with green lawns and flower beds. The few ornamental pillars in the park were relics of an ancient Turkish invasion. The open air theatre which screened only Hindi and Iranian films was at the crossroads where the main avenue met the Dubai highway. Next to it was the shopping arcade Spinnes, Jashmal etc. mainly meant for Westerners. That was the picture of downtown Sharjah in olden days.

Labor office stood next to the Police station. It was mandatory for job seekers to register their names at the labor office. And that set the ball rolling. Very early in the morning aspirants would assemble on the lawns of the labor office and wait for the arrival of the military vehicles from Royal Air Force and Trucial Oman Scouts. Recruiting officials would alight from those vehicles and then announcements would begin: *One storekeeper, one time keeper, 4 waiters...... Those who have necessary qualification , experience and certificates come forward.....* " . Some where lucky, most others were not so lucky.

With a huge handlebar mustache and piercing eyes, police inspector Abdullah Ubaid, was the terror of Sharjah. Clad in imposing khaki uniform he would appear from nowhere and growl *Voin Bathacca?. Show your identity card.* At the roar of his jeep, we trembled and scurried to the safety of the narrow alleys and

by-lanes. There were rumors aplenty about him too-
that he was a homosexual, that he would bully
children....

Major Budd of the Royal Air Force was well
known to the residents of Sharjah. With a benign
face and humble smile he would stroll through the
lanes and alleys in the evenings. He would often stop
passersby and chat with them. My friend Abbas who
was a sergeant with the Trucial Oman Scouts
commented -"*Don't be carried away by his courteous
manners. He is a terrible fellow.*" Abbas was obliquely
referring to the Sharjah palace coup that happened
several years ago. It was alleged that Major Budd
was one of the main architects of that coup.

Colonial forces were ever alert to topple rulers who
wouldn't tow the British lines. Getting rid of one
minion and installing another in his place- this
patronage went on all the time. The fate of Sheikh
Saqr, Ruler of Sharjah was no different, that he was
forcibly pushed out was a well known secret. This
happened in 1965. That story was made spicier by
successive narrators.

British Political Agency at Dubai was the nerve centre of power during those days. It was alleged that one evening Sheikh Saqr, ruler of Sharjah was invited to the British quarters for a state dinner . Once inside British premises, the Sheikh was clandestinely separated from his personal protection regiment and the regiment itself was put under arrest. Then at gun point Sheikh Saqr was informed that he was dethroned. It was a meticulously planned and executed coup by the colonial authorities.

Sheikh Saqr was exiled. For a few years he stayed in Cairo. Then to the dismay of Sharjah residents, he returned with his followers to reclaim the throne. This was in 1972 February. Sheikh Saqr captured the palace and wreaked vengeance on his nephew who had colluded with the British and usurped the throne. But Saqr was subdued by the state military backed by colonial forces and subsequently exiled to an undisclosed prison.

Chocking with the smell of gunpowder Sharjah stood numb in that chilly February. Curfew was clamped in the city. Unaware of that I ventured out.

A military vehicle screeched to a halt in front of me. From inside a soldier thundered brandishing a stent gun *Ya Alla Baith* - Terrified I stood rooted to spot.

That year unprecedented hailstorm lashed Sharjah. Light bulbs in parks and streets were shattered, glass windows of houses, offices and other buildings were damaged. Hailstones lay heaped up everywhere. We shivered, we were not particularly fond of cold or winter.

Air Force Camps used to auction old and used foam beds and blankets for throwaway process. We bought those. But as night progressed, cold permeated through the blankets and gnawed at our bones. We then took shelter in the kitchen, lit the stove, sat around its warmth and shared stories. Sahadevan uncle who had fought in the Indo-China war recounted his adventures in the snow clad Himalyas. Pullan Babu, enacted folk songs; lanky Vijayan entertained us with stories slightly lewd and finally we all broke into bawdy ballads.

Thus collectively we defended ourselves against the cold.

Our kitchen was managed by Sathindran. One day he closed shop. He admonished us *"Nobody has job, no money, how can I run a kitchen?"*. We were left to starve. Mustache Ravi (so called because he had a huge moustache) managed to get some money and with that we bought huge round tandoori rotis from an Iranian eatery. We soaked the dry rotis in suleimani tea and ate.

And then it was summer time. Sun unleashed its savage fury on us. We had no air conditioner, no fridge. Water stored in huge mud pots was cool enough to quench our thirst. Often we stripped down to our underwears to ward off heat.

With reed mats and cotton pillows we spent summer nights on the terrace. Under the starlit sky, a feeble breeze would lull us to sleep, encourage us to see colorful dreams. At daybreak when dew drops began falling we would roll up the mats and get inside the house.

Life was harsh and cruel but that didn't bother us. We had no complaints nor grievances. Because we were young and resilient; we were at the peak of Intoxicating, euphoric youth. And above all we had Hope.

Three

My Reuter Days

I chanced upon the book *"Shifting sands : The British in South Arabia"*, in All Prints Book Shop, Abu Dhabi. The title in red against black background. Authored by David Ledger, my one time boss, the book gives a historic perspective of British dealings in Southern Arabia, now Yemen. Ledger was the Intelligence Officer with the British Political Agency stationed at Aden and later became the personal advisor of the Ruler of Fujairah, one of the Trucial States. The short biographical note stated that the author had retired and was living with his family in a ranch in Dartmoor.

Galloping into the past, I retrieve several portraits of David Ledger- administrator, diplomat, lawyer, journalist . In the pages of the book he attempts a seemingly dispassionate dissection of the turbulent years in South Arabia. About the British policy he admits : *something about South Arabia (that) was not quite right*. It was said that people of Aden once welcomed the visiting Prince of Wales with placards that read *"Tell Daddy we are happy with the British rule"*. Under the British Aden was a thriving market city. Ledger concludes the book by quoting a 1982 incident- the experience of a European traveler stranded in Aden without his baggage. The visitor was astonished to find the shops and emporiums practically empty. All he could get was a pair of drab serge suits made in some unnamed factory in the Eastern bloc. Ledger writes that the locals felt *"It was so much more comfortable when the British were here."*

Like any typical British citizen, David Ledger was a nationalist and a proud imperialist. It was the seventies and sporadic Naxal movement in India had grabbed global attention. He would look at us and ask deridingly "Are you Naxalites?" He came to know of my leftist leanings from Divakaran, my colleague. From then on Ledger made it a habit to tease me. His taunting question still echoes in my ears: *"So tell me, for your salary you are grateful to Mao or to me?"*

I joined Reuters' Bulletin in a cold January. The News agency occupied three rooms in a building which had a total of 5 or 6 rooms. At the far end of the corridor sat Mr Turner, the Editor, middle aged, short tempered and slightly feminine in his gestures. In the central courtyard stood a tall iron pole, the communication tower. A cable drawn from the pole was connected to the office tele-printer which never slept. A Japanese off-set printer spewed out A4 size sheets, which were collated and stitched together to form the bulletin. Reuters Bulletin was one of the first newspapers to enter and fulfill the requirements of the civilized society of the Persian gulf. Two vehicles loaded with latest copies of the bulletin would leave the Sharjah office by 1.00AM; one headed for Dubai and the other for Abu Dhabi.

We were just a handful of staff, mostly Indians (Keralites to be precise) and Pakistanis. Suleiman and Saif were drivers and Shaban the youngster was the newspaper boy. Ledger knew Turner, Suleiman, Saif and Shaban from his Yemeni days. These Yemeni Arabs belonged to the Hadarim tribe. I would often see them huddled together and chewing khat, a special

71

kind of intoxicating green leaves. It was rumored that coca cola enhanced the effect. Khat shrubs are native to Yemen and Ethiopia. Once South Yemen government banned the use of khat which resulted in unprecedented flow of vehicles towards the north Yemen border. The controversial ban was later withdrawn.

Ledger was stationed at Dubai. Every evening he would drive down to Sharjah to discuss the latest news and developments with our editor. Turner, in turn would collect, cut and categorize the spool spit out by the tele-printer. He would match the contents with the nine pm BBC News, and ensure that there were no omissions. Any news item even remotely connected to communism elicited a curse from Turner *"Communists , those bastards."* Perhaps because he had to flee from the bloody communist revolution in Aden.

My duty hours began in the afternoon coinciding with the call for the *asr* prayer and ended well after midnight. By the time I walked back to my lodge, the roads would be deserted. Those days almost every Arab house in Sharjah had watch dogs. They would bark and charge at me. Patrolling police vehicles too would stop and demand to see my *bathaca*. Eventually I became a familiar figure for all of them. Powerful light beams of Royal Air Force made the sky luminous and the fog transparent. I would glide through the gossamer curtain to my shelter.

Thus my days got entangled with the alphabets spit out by the tele-printer. When Gamal Abdel Nasser died, Sharjah mourned and took out a silent procession through the streets. A few of us joined the procession to express our share of condolence. Later the Arab-Israeli war broke out. In cafeterias, people crowded in front of televisions. Then the Shah of Iran celebrated the 2500 years of Royal Iran. That day's issue of Reuter's Bulletin hit the stands showering compliments on Shah. Then came the Indo-Pak war. Reuter's Bulletin reported India's victory. This provoked Pakistanis who publicly burnt copies of the Bulletin in Abu Dhabi. That night we overheard Ledger discussing with Turner on the importance of being discrete in news headlines and contents.

Four

The Boat People

Maniettan's tailoring shop was our leisure time den. It was the seventies and the influx of migrant laborers to the gulf coast was at its peak. From Iran, Pakistan and India they came in overcrowded boats and landed at Dibba, Kalbha or Khor Fakkan, coastal hamlets of Sharjah. Keralites formed the single largest group of this migrant flood. One could spot them from afar- soiled clothes, unsteady walk, dazed look. Maniettan would chuckle " Oh! What a windfall!"

An unusual bond of camaraderie held old and new migrants together. Old timers , like Kumarettan sympathized with the plight of the newly arrived forlorn brethren. In Sharjah Kumarettan's lodge was famous for its "open door policy". The lodge provided shelter and food to the helpless fortune hunters. Sure, they were expected to pay back but then only after getting a steady job. Alas, many took advantage of Kumarettan's generosity and conveniently forgot to repay.

Almost everyday we would hear unsubstantiated tragic tales of launches and boats capsized at the sea. I thumb through the faded entries in my diary.

"February 22, 1970. - A very tragic incident. A boat carrying migrants from Kerala capsized near Rasal Khyma and 50 people drowned."

But despite such disasters the migrant flow continued unabated, like the waves in the sea. Once Sharjah authorities took into custody a boat with nearly 200 illegal migrants from India. They were jailed for a couple of days and then sent back home in the very same boat. Unfortunately the vessel capsized and sank just off the coast of Sharjah, none survived.

> Swept ashore are
> Infinite gifts.
> Froth, pearls, seashells
> Also skeletal remains
> Of unknown migrants drowned in the sea.
> (-Badr Shakir al Sayyab :The Rain Song)

Much later when I read these lines of Sayyab, I felt a shiver run through me. Despite the obvious peril of crossing the seas in small unseaworthy vessels, thousands dared. Their tragic adventures remain unrecorded. Neither the identity of the victims nor their exact count will ever be known. Because Persian Gulf had not yet become the favored destination of celebrities like politicians, poets and artists.

Quite unexpectedly one fine day Maniettan too packed his bags and announced "Friends, let us hope for the best" and disappeared. We wished him well. Someone whispered that he was planning to sneak into Abu Dhabi.

Abu Dhabi was rich, oil exports had increased and with it employment opportunities also had opened up. But entering Abu Dhabi was not easy because of tough travel restrictions even for people from other Trucial States. And as ill luck would have it, Maniettan's motor boat was intercepted by the Abu Dhabi coast guards. The illegal passengers were taken into custody and jailed. After a week of merciless thrashing they were released and sent back to Sharjah.

Maniettan returned with a swollen face and a body beaten black and blue by police. He resumed his tailoring work, with downcast eyes filled with despair.

Five

Where winds erase footprints

In 1971 United Arab Emirates came into existence. With that gulf states lost the British Protectorate status. That very day Iran captured three strategically important islands of Sharjah, which lay in the Hormuz strait. Sharjah boiled, protesters poured into the streets, violent mob destroyed Iranian banks.

Trucial Oman Scouts which till then functioned under the supervision of the British authorities was restructured as the Defense Force of UAE. All institutions associated with and attached to the old Trucial Oman Scouts and the Royal Air Force were closed down. British troops stationed at Sharjah were evacuated. Roars and rumblings of British Air Force planes could no more be heard.

Then the exodus began. The entire migrant labor population, now rendered jobless, began moving from Sharjah towards Abu Dhabi. Sharjah became a deserted city, dry and forlorn. Around this time David Ledger too disappeared under mysterious circumstances. It was rumored that Ledger got involved in cross border smuggling of liquor. When news came that a consignment of his was intercepted on the borders of Saudi Arabia, he conveniently disappeared. There were several other stories too. Whatever be the truth, Ledger never again returned to UAE.

I too bid adieu to Sharjah. Crossing deserts, ascending and descending the hilly terrain I too moved to Abu Dhabi. Years later I came across old copies of the red capped Reuter's Bulletin in the Archives department of Abu Dhabi. Records of events and incidents that invoked memories of bygone days.

Like the poet who penned the Golden Odes, I too lament. Many of those with whom I shared space and time in Sharjah are no more. Sahadevan uncle, Pullan Babu, Vijayan, Ravi...... . Babu and Vijayan chose to end their lives. Ravi couldn't survive a heart attack. A Bedouin folk song echoes in my heart-

> I shall weep for you
> So long as the nightingales sing,
> So long as the stars remain awake
> for the night traveler.

> (*Imr ul Qais-:The Golden Odes* **)**

Sand dunes keep shifting with the tempest of time. Time has erased much of the old Sharjah. Town authorities demolished Ahmed Saleh's white mansion, our lodge. Reuter's News Bulletin has been elbowed out by several other news agencies equipped with latest technology. On her part Sharjah too has shed her coyness and morphed into an ultra modern city with boulevards, flyovers and high-risers. In the global context it is now known as the Cricket City.

> Stay! Let us weep, while memory tries to trace
> The long-lost fair one's sand-girt dwelling-place;

Dubai Puzha

Though the rude winds have swept the sandy plain,
Still some faint traces of that spot remain.
(Imrul Qais : Golden Odes)

Didn't someone say that distance and time bestow
beauty on everything?   ■

Oh Desert!
I have searched the world without finding,
A land more barren, Love more pure,
A rage more fierce than yours.
Oh Desert !

I come back to you
I dally in your night web of mystery
Breathing the soft wind of Najid
The fragrance of Araar
In you I live for poetry and Moon

(Ghazi Al Gosaibi - Desert)

ABU DHABI
Widening Horizons

One

Corniche

To escape the claustrophobic life inside air-conditioned concrete buildings, we would flee outdoors, to the Corniche beach. A balustrade of ornamental silvery arches skirted the Corniche road. Colorful glass domes on top of the arches housed light bulbs. Paved footpaths, cool green lawns and kaleidoscopic fountains, trees in full bloom, flower beds, butterflies, birds – all these enhanced the beauty of the surroundings. During evenings, we would stretch ourselves on the green lawn and stare at the sky, at the floating, white fluffy clouds. When it grew dark, the dazzling splendor of the city lights would lit up the sky. Stars hesitated to appear in such glare, even the few which dared looked dim.

Sweating profusely during the summer and wearing woolens during chilly winter we walked along the

Corniche beach. Often we would wander aimlessly, picking up and nibbling wild berries fallen from roadside trees or shake and force thorny bushes to drop some. Such futile and silly attempts to drive away the drudgery and monotony of migrant life.

Beyond the ramp of arches, parallel to the Corniche lay the long breakwater embankment . Confined between the Corniche beach and the embankment, sea flowed like a river. The embankment had rows and rows of date palms, parks and other recreational facilities. The palm leaves swayed in the wind as if inviting people to a new fun filled life. Viewed from the embankment , the skyline of Abu Dhabi city had the haughtiness of Manhattan, someone said.

Cycling along the bike tracks, walking and running along the sidewalks, rolling and playing in the green lawns, our children grew up. When sharp thorns of the palm trees punctured their balloons, they cried aloud and insisted for new ones. Fun and frolic added joyous colors to their carefree childhood. Sitting on the stone steps leading to the waterfront, my wife and I made plans to transplant our lives back to Kerala. Below, streaks of silver moonlight played on the waves as small fishing boats paddled by. Arab music wafted across from the distant tourist dhows taking passengers for a fun trip to the outer sea. Far away, the lights of Mina beamed strong and bright.

We routinely led our outstation guests, some of them famous others not so famous to the Corniche. Corniche became the backdrop of several of our precious memories. Like the moment when our camera captured the melancholy face of Padmanabhan(3). He was standing close to the dwarf palms, in front of the Hilton Hotel. Sky was overcast, wind blew furiously and raindrops fell. Padmanabhan's mind was equally turbulent because of an unsavory incident that had happened the previous day. "I am very sensitive ", he said. "Yes," I agreed, " artists are made that way". I also remember strolling down the Corniche sidewalk with ONV(4). How charmed he was to listen to *Yara when smiles* a poem set in traditional style.

When yara laughs
The pigeons softly coo
And Fairuz sings for the lovers,
The wedding day is full of gaiety and joy

(Ghazi Al Gosaibi :And when yara smiles)

It seems just yesterday that we spent time with Khader(5) on the Corniche beach as he regaled us with the lighter moments of his life . And then the amusing sight of Ramakrishnan(6) and his wife jumping up in the air to reach for the yellow bunches of dates…

Unknown to myself, the crimson sunset of the Corniche beach had become an obsession from the very beginning of my sojourn at Abu Dhabi. The vast unbound sea had the power to pacify the agitated minds of migrants. During those bachelor days, leaning on the ramp or sitting on the wooden benches, we would gaze at the horizon. Hope for a better future outweighed the agonies of the present. We would linger on the beach even after sunset. The western sky would acquire a faint glow from the burning pits of Das Island. Ravi my friend once declared " If I can save

100,000 rupees, I will pack up and go back home."
The dreams of his near and dear ones depended on
his earnings. As darkness deepened and city lights came
on, we would return to Ravi's room, pull out a scotch
bottle from underneath his cot, pour into glasses and
sip. As alcohol rushed through the nerves, eyes
reddened, conversation became intense and silence
deeper. Thus we would live through one more night
to begin a new day....

Ravi, finally went home. But that story didn't have
a happy ending. We soon heard that he died of a heart
attack leaving behind unfulfilled dreams and promises.
I sat numb on the wooden bench under the almond
tree in the Corniche beach and shed tears for him.
Later I had my own share of grief to cope up with.
The realization that our new born son would forever
be our sorrow, broke our heart. My wife was
inconsolable. For years Corniche walkways got
drenched in our tears. Our son grew up in his own
special way , amusing himself throwing shoes and toys
in to the water......

Again I sought solace from the surroundings-
blossoms, birds, breeze. From the vaults of the sky

the wise old man of Arabian folktales came down and comforted me " Son, is there a single chalice without its share of sorrow?"

Two

Madinat Zaid

Madinat Zaid had the unmistakable stamp of a refugee colony. Crowded, cramped and miserable. Arab houses scattered in disorderly fashion, narrow lanes, dust and smoke from vehicular traffic, stinking heaps of garbage waiting to be cleared, broken sewage pipes, ramshackle houses and filth everywhere. Madinat Zaid was also the escape route from the traffic snarls of the city. Sandwiched between Electra street and Jawazat Road, Madinat Zaid was earlier an exclusively Arab residential area with typical Arab style houses sporting courtyard and compound wall. Arab owners later built annexes and extensions and rented these out to migrant workers. Later when government built villas for its citizens in new upcoming suburbs, Arab families moved out and Madinat Zaid became a ghetto of third world immigrants. Or to be frank Madinat Zaid became a slum, a shanty town of Abu Dhabi.

The houses had brick walls but roofs were made of asbestos or plywood. When it rained, though it was a rare occurrence, roof leaked mercilessly. Wall mounted air conditioners dripped and growled nonstop, radiating heat outside.

Migrant workers, groups of frustrated men, lived in those rooms. Forlorn and orphaned in appearance they left for work at dawn and returned to the rooms at dusk. They would stay confined within the air-conditioned rooms trying to focus on the television screen, eating chicken curry and khubz, or drink or listen to *kathupattukal* songs highlighting the agony of lovelorn pairs fated to stay separate. This was their maddeningly monotonous routine day after day. At times, they would roam aimlessly in the shopping malls or crowded market places. Like sex-starved sailors at sea or soldiers at warfront, their eyes would lust on every female figure they saw. But then they were duty bound family men who regularly sent letters and money home. During the first week of every month they lined up at bank counters or offices of loan sharks to remit money home. Every year or perhaps every two years they visited their families with suitcases bursting at the seams. They spent a large part of their annual savings to pay for excess baggage and/or bribes. After a brief vacation they would return, rejuvenated; back to the grey skies of Abu Dhabi, back to the shoddy Madinat Zaid.

Majority of the residents of Madinat Zaid were migrants from Indian subcontinent, East Africa, coastal areas of Red sea or the Mediterranean. They had valid passports and home address. There were a few from Palestine, with no legal documents.

When transplanted in foreign soil, migrants initially suffer a culture shock. Eventually they learn to adapt to even extreme situations; they learn to coexist with sewage rats and cats rummaging through stinking garbage piles.

Madinat Zaid boasted of a Kerala Arts Centre. This used to be the venue for theatre festivals, concerts, dances and cultural debates. We shared our sincere concerns about the third world. Ideas and ideologies on revolution, counter revolution, modernization and development clashed there. Members were familiar with Lorca, Neruda, Marquez, Castro, Camus… In front of the Arts Centre stood an ancient mosque. Whenever its loudspeaker announced prayer time, our heated discussions would grind to a halt and we would observe 5 minutes silence as a mark of respect.

Three

Under the Jujube Tree

My little daughter gathered all the sheep droppings scattered in the courtyard and showed to us proudly : *Look how beautiful these seeds are….*

With my wife and little daughter , I spent five years in a rented accommodation in Madinat Zaid, close to the Jawazat Road. We divided the spacious majlis into a drawing room and a bedroom. The house belonged to Fatima , an Arab widow. She and her three sons lived in the main house. Abdul Khader, the eldest was an officer with the Abu Dhabi airport facility. The second one was a high school student who always wore

91

canvas shoes and sports clothes and was crazy about football. He was the main player of the Al Ahali sports Club. We nicknamed him *Mr Koora,* Mr Football. The youngest was a shy kid who went to school in the morning and returned home by afternoon.

Fatima was widowed several years ago. She brought up her children with great difficulty, working as a domestic help in rich Arab houses and selling perfumes. This piece of information was provided to us by Usman, who ran a provision store in Jawazat Road. Fatima had Iranian roots and the family spoke Persian at home. Whenever her Iranian relatives visited, we received a share of pistachio and a slab of cardamom flavored halwa. Fatima used to grill fish in the courtyard and the smell would fill the air. During festivals she would send large trays filled with grilled fish, dry fruits, nuts and pudding….. We accepted the offerings with due respect and gratitude. It was unthinkable to refuse, because that would have been an insult. We would whisper among ourselves - *too much salt in the fish, too cold pudding , not clean enough…* Still we would eat whatever we could and dump the rest.

A jujuba tree showing off its thorns and tiny leaves stood in our courtyard. During summer months, the berries would ripen and fall in the courtyard. Fatima's sheep forever tied to the jujuba tree reminded me of a novel by the famous Malayalam writer Bashir(7) . My toddler daughter used play in the courtyard in her underwear. Fatima would admonish my wife- *a girl child shouldn't walk around without proper clothes.*

My friend Raghunathan who worked for the horticultural department , presented me with a wagonful of plants, together with a roll of iron fencing. We barricaded a part of the courtyard with the fencing and planted the saplings within. We nursed and nurtured the plants with water and manure and the saplings thrived. We were proud of our own little green patch. Our next door neighbor had a few cows formidable in size. Those animals used to gaze longingly at our greenery with melancholy eyes because their usual food source was the garbage heap nearby. One day the cows breached our fence and ate up all the plants. Our little garden became just a memory.

Those days we used to receive strange phone calls. These calls were targeted at housewives, especially when the husbands were away at work. Callers were Keralites for sure. Some would sweet talk, others will use most obscene language , a few others would directly invite for sleeping together- manifestations of suppressed libido. It wasn't difficult to get the caller details. For a fee of 300 dirhams, Etisalat, Abu Dhabi the telecom dept. would provide the required information. Thus some were caught jailed and deported. Most of the affected parties didn't want to get into the maze of police and court, hence just ignored such calls. Kerala Samajam organized a seminar and the main topic of discussion was such prank calls. One lady activist implored the men to introspect. Just around that time, Abdul Azeez, a Maharashtrian Indian was beheaded in public because he was the main accused in the molestation and murder of an Arab girl child. Shariat Law stipulated beheading for such crimes.

And then it was Khader's marriage. Fatima's food trays filled our dining table. Guests thronged the

courtyard. Music band arrived in two vehicles. An evening of singing, clapping and dancing. Men and women participated in these festivities. Hijras danced with feminine movements.

Khader's bride's name was Salama. Light eyed and plump, she had done schooling upto tenth standard. In the evenings under the jujuba tree she would chat with my wife in not so perfect English. Khader had paid *meher* to her father. Meher is the cash groom pays to the bride's father. In the eventuality of a divorce, this money comes in handy for the woman to shape her future. Bride's father is expected to be the trustee, but in reality, many fathers squander away the money or use it to procure an additional bride for themselves.

Once Salama asked my wife "Sister, have you heard of Bangkok? It is a very bad place, isn't it?" Salama's eyes were moist. Khader along with two of his friends was planning to go to Bangkok for two weeks. He refused to take Salama along. We witnessed Bangkok rising up as a dark cloud and raining down marital discord in Arab homes.

During July and August, hot winds lashed the city. Yellow dates would ripen, drop off the bunch and decay beneath the trees, filling the air with intoxicating sweet smell. Walking along the Diwan Amir Road, we would inhale the heavy, sweet smell; we would jump in the air to reach for the bunches, our footwear would get enmeshed in the syrupy mess and we would slip.

Abu Dhabi city has changed a lot since then. Arab families have been relocated to new villas in the outskirts such as Al-Sab, Al-Batain, Umm Al Nar. Madinat Zaid too has undergone a makeover. It is no longer a filthy locality. Neatly laid out roads, paved walkways, high-risers, shopping malls, spacious, fully airconditioned vegetable, fish and meat markets.

Madinat Zaid is no longer a shanty town, it is a posh locality.

Four

Inheritance of Loss

Suad Randisi was my friend, neighbor and colleague. She was a Palestinian belonging to the orthodox

Christian church. We went to work together, either she knocked at my door or I waited for her. Whenever I was overburdened with work she would offer to help. We worked at the busy market branch of the bank. During leisure time we would discuss politics, literature, poetry and local news. She frankly shared her views.

-I mailed so many of my poems to Al Etihad. They refuse to publish a single one. Perhaps because I am a Palestinian.

She would share her disappointment with me. Palestinians held the general feeling that every Arab city marginalized them, alienated then. I reminded her of Rimbaud(8) to tease her

Then Rimbaud became a slave trader, he stopped writing poetry

When he cast nets to trap the black lions of Ethiopia, he stopped writing poetry.

Because Rimbaud was an honest man.

Later many poets became slave traders but they continued to write poems

Their poems adorned the Sultan's palace, as door or window frames, tables and carpets

Still they continued to write poems......

I taunted her " Won't it be better for you to be honest like Rimbaud and stop writing poetry? Having fled from the rough and rude realities of your homeland, you are now enjoying the comforts of another capital city. What would be the message of your poems? Will they too become the doors and windows of Sultan's palace?"

My sneer was intentional, but she refused to take the bait. I reminded her of Dr Habash. Or was it she who mentioned him?

Dr Habash was her neighbor and family friend in Amman. He ran a clinic in the city. One fine day, he closed down the clinic, jumped into the thick of Palestinian movement and founded the left wing organization Popular Front for the Liberation of Palestine (PFLP). He was an extraordinary individual, she said and showered praises on him. While discussing Palestine, she would often cite the gospel **(9)**

"But those husbandmen said among themselves, This is the heir; come let us kill him, and the inheritance will be ours. And they took him and killed him and cast him out of the wineyard"

Suad had no recollection of her lost inheritance of the vineyards of the West Bank. When her family crossed the Jordan river to the safety of Amman, she was a little child, oblivious of the happenings around her. Prior to departure, her family had sold their ancestral property, and with that money they could maintain a reasonably good life style in Amman. Suad married Khader, who was studying for medicine in Damascus. Later when Khader got appointment with the Health Department of Abu Dhabi, they both moved to this city. Government provided them with a spacious flat complete with all modern furnishings and amenities. The couple didn't have children. Suad dissipated that regret in multiple ways. She wrote poems, went for swimming, played tennis, and spent time in kitchen. She was an excellent cook. Her dinner dishes often appeared next day on our office dining table. Cheese khubuz, cookies, dolmas, cakes, Turkish coffee..... *Look, we from the Middle East are the best cooks. No other region can boast of as many dishes as we have. After all we have the rich heritage of having produced two prophets"*

Khader and Suad adopted Sayyida, a distant relative. Sayyida, a beautiful girl of eighteen was enrolled at the American University of Beirut. She would visit them during vacations. She was very fond of children On Christmas eve she would visit us and give presents to my children.

Every year Suad and Khader vacationed abroad. Europe, America, India......

In search of the roots of Orthodox Christian Church, they went to Moscow. They visited Cremlin, Gorbachev was at the fag end of his political career. Their next trip was to the West Bank, in search of their own roots. They were excited about the impending reunion with relatives who had stayed back.

Thus after several decades they crossed the Jordan River and set foot in the West Bank. .She extended her leave for another two weeks. Our Operations Manager was a British national with strong anti-Palestine views. He would grimace at the mention of the word " Palestine." Suad was well aware of his attitude. She often told me " He is the successor of Wingate" (10) . Suad didn't report for duty even after the expiry of the extension. Operations Manager took the opportunity to sack her citing laws and bylaws. Finally Suad returned and pleaded her case vociferously.

"Sir, West Bank is an Israel occupied territory. Timely postal and telecommunication links are virtually impossible. I had been waiting for your confirmation. Iit isn't easy to send messages across. West Bank is not Europe or America- it is a dark region of barbaric laws."

Her words fell on deaf ears. Then the usual ritual of farewell…. She was my colleague for 15 years. Before leaving she whispered to me Leila Khaled's words: *"Killing the rightful heir, they threw us out, the British gave them full support. In Persian Gulf now, we, the Palestinians are the foreigners not the British or Americans"*

Five

The Irony of Sand Roses

Samaran sent me Sand Roses. *'When you dig deep churning the blistering hot sand with the bulldozer, suddenly sand roses reveal themselves. Like the exquisite artwork of a unique*

104

sculptor, or like an elegant poem. Sand roses with a thousand petals".

Sand roses are as hard and strong as steel. This stunning piece of art by Mother Nature takes years of incubation. It is as if the desert is making a strong statement- *what if I am harsh and barren, I can create beauty.* Samaran's gift adorns my drawing room and constantly reminds me of those who wilt in the desert to flourish in life ..

Tall buildings, paved walkways, tree lined broad boulevards, foreign cars, parks- I found Arabian cities beautiful and life very comfortable …Yet I couldn't help writing home

"Somehow surviving in the biting cold and scorching heat….."

Hollow words Cliché ridden sentences sound hollow. Old habits are hard to shed; later I was indeed ashamed of myself.

Samaran was employed in the oil fields of Asab, in the sprawling deserts of Abu Dhabi. There night and day oscillated between extreme temperatures: icy frost and blistering heat. Workers lived in air-conditioned tents. Outside wind blew, nonstop, fiery hot in summer and bone chilling in winter. Just sand, as far as one can see. Ephemeral sand dunes disappeared and reappeared elsewhere. Just like the harsh realities of life. Samaran Tharayil, summarized it thus :

> Earth like an inverted bowl,
> Up in the sky a piece of cloud
> Casts its dark shadow on the earth

Western region of Abu Dhabi is oil rich. Once I travelled up to Liwa oasis. What an amazing landscape, or should I say sandscape? Miles and miles of sand dunes . Beyond that lay the *Rub' Al Khali* literally the *Empty Quarter* .

Samaran wrote :*Tar topped black roads end at Liwa. Beyond that only windswept desert as far as one can see. Vehicles must follow the tracks marked by black rubber tubes. Before driving out drivers will reduce air pressure in the tire. Huge tankers and trucks with 8 or 10 pairs of wheels can easily drive through the desert tracks. They connect the oil fields with the outside world. As soon as a vehicle departs from an oil depot, radio message is sent to the next halt. If the vehicle fails to report within the stipulated time, helicopters begin search for the vehicle and its driver... lost in the desert .....perhaps still alive or.....Once an experienced driver made the mistake of stepping out of the cool comfort of the driver's cabin. Feet on scorching sand 60 0r 70 degC. overhead sun ablaze like a fire ball, he collapsed in no time...* Such terrifying stories....

Reading Samaran's letters were like thumbing through a picture book - scurrying wild rabbits, snakes hunting for prey, jackals howling in the night.. drifting sands mercilessly pulling down unsuspecting animals and human beings ..... wind blowing nonstop, at times as sand blast. The wretchedness of a migrant worker, cursed to live alone within the confines of a tiny tent was evident in those letters, I could feel it.

Decades ago Wilfred Thesiger **(11)**, who explored the wilderness of the desert wrote " *....only changing temperature marks the passage of the year..a bitter desiccated land which knows nothing of gentleness or ease Yet men have lived here since earliest time.*"

When Prince Charles came visiting, the desert people welcomed him with their own music and dance. Samaran wrote despite the dry, barren ambience, art and culture survives in the desert. Their folk songs are oral traditions, handed down from generation to generation. When they sing in guttural sounds, lips don't move.

Very often officers visited the oil fields for inspection associated operations. Bosses didn't stir out of the cool comfort of the air-conditioned vehicles and it always fell to the lot of the employees of the lowest cadre to descend into the fire pits. Samaran was disturbed at this inequality at work place. The fact that most of them were Keralites pained him even more.

Loneliness of the desert woke up the storyteller in him. But his stories were all set in the lush green villages of his homeland. Some of his stories were published in magazines, and earned both brickbats and bouquets. From Arabian cities my voice resonated over the radio transmitters and reached out to him wilting in the desert. He didn't want to write about the desert or the migrants. *All that must wait till I finally return to my homeland*, he said. *Distance endows magnificence to a scenery, as does time to memories* - did he say that too? After two decades in the desert plains, now he is stationed in the city of Dubai. When would be his homecoming?

Those who willingly wither in the desert to flourish in life.

*Sa*nd roses are smiling at me.

Six

The Third World

From one shelter to another. That was the frustrating aspect of Abu Dhabi life. Rental accommodations were not easy to find. House owner, invariably an Arab would come over as and when he pleased and hike up the rent. With no other option, we would hunt or a cheaper accommodation. Muscular *Pathans*, helped us move our furniture and kitchenware. Rough and rude, they broke our glass paneled almirah, smashed our crockery and then argued vehemently for more wages than initially agreed upon. Tempers rose, with that our blood pressure too.

One such move led me to Muroor. In Arabic, *Muroor* means a transport office or check-post. Naturally the neighborhood too borrowed the name. Trucks and jeeps loaded with cargo intended for San'a

and Ta'izz lay lined up there waiting for permits. Yemeni families who had fled from the communist revolution and migrants from Kenya, Somalia and Zanzibar were my neighbors, many of them were my colleagues too. Daily I woke up to the music of southern Arabia and eastern Africa together with a cacophony of languages: Arabic, Sahili, Somali... I would wonder have I moved to the East African coast?

The bay that enwrapped Abu Dhabi city had made shallow inlets not far from our backyard. Mangroves flourished there and became a rich breeding ground for a variety of fish and crab. On Fridays and holidays we would get together at this cove, catch fish and hunt for crabs. Then would make a feast of fried fish and curried crab and wash it down with cold beer.

To get to our offices in the city and back we used public transport. Share taxies were also available. One day while returning from work, I had a strange experience. Seated inside the bus, I was immersed in the *Khaleej Times*, and didn't particularly notice when an Egyptian came and sat in front of me. A little while later he called out to me:

-Are you an Indian?

-Yes, I nodded.

-Then tell me why in your great country Muslims are being killed mercilessly?

I was aghast and looked around. My fellow passengers were mostly Egyptians, Somalians and Palestinians. They were all listening to the interloper. After a moment's hesitation I protested.

-No, that is not quite true. Well, there might be occasional communal tensions and riots . But our government is secular and our constitution guarantees it.

-Blatant lie!. In your country communal riots happen every day. And our innocent Muslim brethren are killed.

The guy was hysterical and continued the tirade against India and everything Indian.

-   You call yours a civilized country, where a single cow can hold up the traffic in a metro city for hours?

I thought it prudent to keep quiet, Why make a scene in a public place?.

Next day on my way to office, a Palestinian neighbor, who had spent almost a year in New Delhi befriended me. He had witnessed the previous day's event. He consoled me

- yours is indeed a secular country. We Palestinians too had dreamt of a secular state where Muslims, Christians and Jews would live in peace. But when Zionists began importing Jews from all over the globe, our idea of secularism failed

Yousuf- that was his name- had earlier worked with the Palestinian Mission in New Delhi, he was a member of one of the many delegations that met Indira Gandhi.

-We hate Egyptians. With Camp David Treaty they cheated the entire Arab world. Now they are the American Agents in the middle east. An average Egyptian from Cairo is useless, but an Alexandrian is more trustworthy.

In school I had learned about Egypt. Cradle of an ancient civilization like India. Then in modern times the close association of Nehru and Nasser in implementing the Non-aligned movement along with Tito. On the surface there was no room for animosity between the two countries or countrymen. But I guess Egyptians resented the overwhelming presence of Indians in the gulf because both were competitors in the job market. Indians , on their part painted Egyptians in dark colors. Egyptian became the villain in offices and public spaces. Rumors about an Indian patient who almost died at the hands of an Egyptian doctor.. so on and so forth…

Yousuf, though employed temporarily with the Abu Dhabi Electricity department, actually worked for a secret Palestinian organization, or so it was alleged. He criticized Arafat openly and sharply. *"Oh He just dines with sheikhs in their palaces…..."* One day Yousuf disappeared, I never met him again. I would remember him whenever Palestine shot into prime time news. For example when the Munich massacre happened; when King Hussein of Jordan took military action against Palestinians; when Palestinian rebels set fire to a civilian plane in Jordan deserts; when Lebanon was

114

in turmoil….. …. Walking home cutting across the saline marshland, I wondered- *Yousuf- was that his real name?-* To me he was a stranger whose homeland was in the grip of locusts and tragedies.

Our bus stop in Muroor had a name- Hadarim. Because migrant workers from Hadramuth region of south Yemen were the predominant settlers in that locality. Khasim, Abdi, Mehmood, Meigog- all were from East African coast, my neighbours and my colleagues at the bank. They preferred to stay away from the buzz of the city. I often went with them to African eateries and ate mutton soup and noodles. Soup was a huge piece of boiled meat- almost half a kilo- and its stock. We interacted freely taunting and teasing each other. My uncharitable comments on their apelike anatomical features incited them and they in turn mimicked the *Malabarian* mannerisms. My observations that after Ethiopia, Yemen and Afghanistan it was now Africa's turn for Spring Thunder were not in the least welcome; so I branded them reactionaries. Khasim gave me a lengthy lecture refuting communism.

Time moved on. We climbed several steps in our career ladder. In many countries political winds changed directions. Mengistu fled Ethiopia, Aden city was taken over by north Yemeni forces and in Afghanistan Najibulla was displaced. But our camaraderie continued; we often got together, shared jokes, mulled over old times and laughed freely.

Somalia was experiencing one of the worst famines in its history. This was compounded by tribal war. Television screens relayed pictures of emaciated, malnourished children. Disturbed, we would switch off TV sets, but those images haunted us and robbed us of sleep and peace of mind. While Nadine Gordimer's writings acquainted me with the harsh realities of a racially divided Africa, its people and politics, Somalian situation showcased yet another kind of human tragedy.

I asked Mehmood about organizing relief funds for the Somalian children. He wasn't interested. Because in Hargeisa, the region to which he belonged, everything was fine he said.

On the other hand Meigag was very much disturbed. For years he hadn't been -or rather couldn't go- to his hometown. Pirates were waiting to clean up his family because his uncle was a member of the deposed Siad Barre cabinet. That was the reason they fled from Somalia. Meigag's briefcase contained documents- meticulous plans for bringing back the revolution in Somalia. In free time he made photocopies of these documents. Once in a while a few sheets would escape the fold and land on our desks. There were plans for reviving the traditional economy of Somalia which depended on bananas, cattle and shepherds.

And then America became the dream destination for the citizens of the third world. My Somali friends Mehmood and Meigag waited patiently at the Emigration counter of American Embassy at Abu Dhabi. My collegue Sarah and her husband too joined queue. At the fag end of the line I could spot Jacob George and his family.

I recollect the lines of the Malayali poet, Ayyappa Panikkar who looked for the heart line in the map of America:

117

On top of an elegant hill stands a cross
With a paper heart neatly pinned on it
"Oh Today is Christmas" a scrawl across
As if added as an afterthought

Seven
About a Marriage of Convenience

Telephone rang. A rather unfamiliar voice on the other end.

-Good Morning Mr Das, this is Rosie.

Rosie? It took me a full minute to place her. Ah, yes Rosie, wife of Ahmed Koori the commercial Manager of our Bank. Ahmed was a *watani*, native of Abu Dhabi and Rosie was from Cochin, Kerala. The couple had 7 children. .

Rosie wanted me to coach her for an upcoming interview with an oil company. *Brush up on accounts,* that is what she said. My surprise knew no bounds. Certainly, there was no need for Rosie to take up a job? Ahmed Koori was rich and had built a palatial house for her in Umm Al Nar. The entire office was invited for the house-warming party. Ahmed took us around and showed every nook and corner of the house. Marble flooring, ornate furniture, costly furnishings, chandeliers …..Such opulence! Rosie could live like a queen. Why would she want a job now? I couldn't resist asking.

-Oh well! I have no peace of mind staying at home. A job will keep my mind engaged. Moreover if I have a job I needn't ask him for every little need of mine.

I agreed to coach her…..

Then she asked

-How is *he* now?

Obviously the reference was to Ahmed Koori. My lips remained sealed. Why should I say anything? Someone might paint me in the shades of Iago.

It was several years ago that Rosie D'Souza came to our bank in search of a job. She had come on visiting visa and its validity had expired, but she had no intention of returning to Kerala. Ahmed Koori managed to get her a job, she worked for a brief while and then we heard that they got married. Rosie converted to Islam and later she left the job.

Rosie was Ahmed's second wife. He had no children from the first marriage and anyway Islam allowed multiple marriages. Between Rosie and Ahmed it was certainly a marriage of convenience. Rosie as no beauty but was very smart and efficient. She delivered seven babies in quick succession and Ahmed celebrated each arrival with us. Ahmed was very popular in office because he was everyone's Man Friday.

-*My driving licence, please help*

-Landlord is asking for huge rent for the flat in Jawasat Road, please make him agree for less.

-My roommate was caught by police, please get him released...

Appeals and demands were varied and myriad and Ahmed would help all. He was a *watani* (native) and hence could easily manage things. Keralites joked, that they have claims on him, after all he has married a Keralite.

While setting annual targets for the bank, our manager a British, would insist "This year the savings deposit must increase by a 100 million". Ahmed would respond " Inshah Allah". *God willing*. Manager would counter impatiently " *Inshah Allah* won't do; the target must be achieved" Ahmed would retort " Sir, we Muslims leave everything to Allah. It is up to him to give or not to give".

Annual celebrations of the bank were western style gala events. These were held in 5 star hotels with drinks, dance followed by dinner. Ahmed would always be the one leading from the front. Rosie too, being of Anglo-Indian origin liked dancing. As dancing progressed, Ahmed would transition from Western style to Arabian folk dance. He also took the initiative to organize family tours and excursions. Once we visited an exclusive farmhouse in Khor Fakkaan. We enjoyed the swimming pool, picked fruits and lemons. Rosie would accompany Ahmed Koori in all such events.

But Ahmed had a weakness for women. That led to cracks in their marital life. Rosie kept tabs on Ahmed

through old friends at the office. She had a hotline with our colleague Cheriyan who fed her with *Breaking News.*

-*His current infatuation is a Bombay girl. He escorts her everywhere. Rosie you must be careful....*

Armed with this information Rosie would confront Ahmed; he would fidget in front of her.

Abbas Mehmood, the public relations manager was a close ally of Ahmed Koori. Abbas often boasted of his gallivants and shared sordid details with us. He would show us love letters from Philippines. Inside would be *lots of kisses* and demand for 50 or 100 dollars for each kiss and finally supplications for a visa at the earliest . Abbas couldn't read or write English. So it fell to one of us to read and reply on his behalf. For this he bothered us often even during office hours. Once I went with Abbas to the City the traffic office. A well dressed, obviously rich Arab lady arrived in a self driven car . She spent a lot of time with Abbas. I was curious: Was she from a Sheikh family? I asked him later. Abbas laughed and replied. *She is a top class prostitute, wants to know why I don't visit her anymore.*

Somehow Abbas managed to be in charge of groups of women from Srilanka and Philippines who arrived in Dubai hoping to be domestic helps. Abbas and Ahmed rented a flat to accommodate these women and lived life Casanova style. All this was known to everyone in the bank. But Ahmed was intrigued how did Rosie get wind of it? That too even the minutest detail? He walked around in the office with his antenna up. I used to meet their son Mohammed once in a while. "Mom and dad quarrel all the time," he said. During one such quarrels it seems Rosie herself blurted out "Yes, Cheriyan gives me the news...."

Ahmed was furious and threatened Cheriyan- " Are you set to ruin my family life? If I put a little pressure, you will lose your job. God forbid, don't force me "

Several months, perhaps several years elapsed after that. Then once again the bank staff went on an excursion; this time to Banas island. It was the private property of the Ruler; needed special permission from the Royal office. Ahmed Koori managed everything.

It took four hours in a Russian boat to reach the island. A scenic place with elegant royal palaces and beautiful gardens. Out in the wilderness groups of gazelles grazed. Human voices scared them away. African giraffes held their head high . There was a bird sanctuary too. Swans, pelicans and a variety of other birds whose names we didn't know had made the island their home. But this time Rosie didn't accompany Ahmed. Instead Ahmed Koori glided past us arm in arm with his fourth bride, as if in a fairyland

Will Rosie be bickering with Ahmed still? I wonder....

I wonder about many other things too- about affluence, about poverty, about the barren desert where the Prophet's Words germinated....

You know how little while we have to stay,
And once departed, may return no more

Ah my beloved, fill the cup that clears
Today of past regrets and future fears-
Tomorrow? –Why tomorrow I may be
Myself with yesterdays seven thousand years

(Rubaiyat of Omar Khayyam 3 and 20)

A DEATH - IN RETROSPECT

Just about a week before his death, Alikka began writing his memoirs. Quite a hurried effort, indeed. Perhaps he had an intuition about his impending death. At that time he was working as a receptionist at the Binunia guest house located in the Ruwais industrial township. The township grew around petrochemical industries which included oil fields, refineries, and gas plants.

Alikka's memoirs begin quite abruptly

"Night 2.00AM. Room number 201 of Binunia guest house. Too disturbed to sleep, I toss and turn in my bed".

The flames from the burning pit might have imparted a reddish glow to the surroundings. And there Alikka was trying to account for 32 years of his life. The 32 long years that he toiled in the scorching desert for the sake of his family.

Dubai Puzha

It was the usual story. Poverty stricken childhood-helpless parents- large family- 4 sisters to be married off. All these factors colluded and pushed Alikka to embark on an agonizing voyage across the seas to the Persian gulf. Alikka had no special skillset to boast of hence fell in the category of casual laborers. He moved from one place to another from one temporary job to another, braving the alien landscape and seasons. It took him years to get his sisters married off but he did it in style. Then he even arranged jobs for his brothers in law and brought them over to the gulf. Filial duties over, he heaved a sigh of relief. In the meanwhile his three daughters and son had grown up. Parental duties stared in his face. But he was not worried, confident that his sisters would definitely help. But that was not to be. His sisters and their husbands had other priorities; they quarreled with Alikka on flimsy grounds and moved away.

Alikka had to start all over again. But age and failing health let him down on many occasions. For years he didn't go home, because he had to save every dirham. Family life became a distant memory, but he wrote home regularly. Affectionate letters along with bank drafts of his meager earnings.

His wife sent an ultimatum : *"I am worried....... at least the eldest must be married off at the earliest. Or else.... we can put an end to our lives".*

Alikka was distraught, begging and borrowing he managed enough money for the marriage of his eldest daughter. But then he had 2 more daughters and a son. He was a spent force, attacks of arthritis, asthma and hypertension conspired to erode his health.

Once a prospective employer asked him:

-How old are you?

-Sixty.

-At this age you should be relaxing with your grandchildren, this job is not for you.

But he needed a job, any job, he was desparate. Finally with great difficulty he managed to get the job of a receptionist in Binunia guest house for a paltry salary. Lonely and broken in spirit and body, he agonized over the absurdity of his life; of the thirty two youthful years spent in the desert for the sake his sisters. They , now rich had distanced themselves from him and his wife considered him irresponsible. Is Life a synonym for selfishness and ingratitude?

Alikka came to see me with his book – "Suggest a suitable title. .. I feel drained, can't think of any".

I read the novelette. Familiar sob story… story of many a Malayalee migrant worker or for that matter any migrant worker ; story of martyrdom for thankless family; told and retold several times in several settings . But I couldn't bring myself to tell all that to Alikka. When I met him next I tried to stall the project .

- "I can suggest a title….. but before that if you can rewrite this.. You know … unusually long sentences…. repetitions…….."

Alikka became impatient. " No, No time for all that… This must reach Editor's desk as it is at the earliest. He is my friend, let him edit it as he pleases" . Then he added as if he had a premonition :" My days are numbered I know for sure. This is my life's story. I can't rewrite this in any other way. My friends and relatives must read this. Especially my sisters….."

132

Alikka's eyes blazed; and then tears rolled down his cheeks. I think I was kind of shaken too. The concluding part of the book flashed across my mind- a bizarre fantasy in which his sisters dance gleefully in front of his dead body.. . ....

That evening we had organized a music program in my flat. Ebrahim Kutty's finger tips could pluck out the most melodious notes from the sitar strings. He had trained for 5 years under a well known maestro in Mumbai. I invited Alikka. Friends arrived with tabla and other instruments. First a round of drinks, then light refreshments. After that we settled down to listen to the verses of Omar Khayyam

You know how little while we have to stay,

And once departed , may return no more

....

Ah my beloved, fill the cup that clears
Today of past regrets and future fears-
Tomorrow? —Why tomorrow I may be
Myself with yesterdays seven thousand years

133

And then notes from the sitar harmoniously blended with the rhythm of the tabla and gently caressed our sense and sensibilities. Melting away all that was harsh and dissonant in our lives, *Raag Darbari* breached the barrier of walls and filled the neighborhood.

Alikka had dozed off to sleep. When I woke him up he looked around in bewilderment. Did I wake him up from a nostalgic dream?

Two days later we received the news that Alikka succumbed to a heart attack. My shock expressed itself as a shriek and moistened my eyes.

K.P. M. Ali that was his full name; For us he was always Alikka, our affectionate elder brother. He was a simpleton, a social activist, an excellent orator. Occasionally he penned a few literary pieces, some of which got published.

Alikka was an enthusiastic member of the Kerala Arts Centre at Madinat Zaid, the shanty town of Abu Dhabi. He had great plans for the centre: to fill the shelves of the library with classics, conduct debates and discussions on art, literature and culture... He worked hard to translate these dreams into reality. He arranged with a publisher in Kerala for the delivery of high quality books. The Reading room overflowed with books and journals; evenings saw lively discussions on a variety of topics. Those were the golden days of Kerala Arts Centre. But dark days soon followed. A new executive committee took over, new rules, autocracy, embezzlement of funds, rigging of elections and misrepresentation of results ...Large sums of money collected from *Snowball* disappeared into the pockets of a few. The services of the hitherto financial auditor(that was me) were summarily rejected. Protesters were bullied into submission... A small dissent group which included Alikka and me was marginalized and we became mute spectators.

The city itself was undergoing expansion and modernization. Madinat Zaid, the eyesore of Abu Dhabi city was razed to the ground. Bulldozers arrived to pull down the Kerala Arts Centre and gobbled up the elegantly bound classics so painstakingly collected by Alikka. Thankfully Alikka was away in New York, serving as a cook for an Arab military official at the UAE embassy. He would write to us long letters- about Hudson river, Manhattan, statue of Liberty, the Brooklyn Bridge- the engineering marvel. He also wrote about capitalism, about black cabdrivers, about mugging…..

After 5 years in New York, the boss and the servant returned to Abu Dhabi and settled in a sprawling flat in Corniche. Unfortunately the boss got entangled in a political or financial quandary and was imprisoned. Alikka continued as the caretaker of the flat. We were staying in a tiny flat in the same neighborhood. Almost every evening we got together to spice up our lives with poetry, anecdotes, stories….. At times Alikka teased our taste buds with machboos, chicken casserole….

One evening Alikka allowed us a peep into his secret treasure- a bagful of old letters, old newspaper and magazine clippings, published and unpublished literary work … collected over a life time and providing a new perspective of the past…..

We often discussed the limits and limitations of a migrant's life. Uncertainty of job, fear and anxiety, trauma of neglect and desertion, complexity of family ties, discords in *long-distance* marital life….. Fully aware that life was getting squeezed into a monotonous mould, many a migrant resigns himself to a soulless existence.

Once he pulled out a sheet from his collection. A brief piece titled "Fear" written by Rahman Vadanappilli.

"Mustafa was a farash (office boy) in the dusty office. His job was to sweep and mop the office and keep it spic and span. As he went about his job, he would cough continuously. Enraged, one day his arbab(boss) thundered: "If you cough once more you will be dismissed." Mustafa was terrified. Dismissal? Oh no! He couldn't afford to be dismissed. His family in Kerala was dependent on the draft he sent every month. He didn't cough any more; the cough just disappeared."

We are like the coconut palms struggling to survive in the desert along side the native date palms, Alikka would say… and recite the Vyloppilli's famous Malayalam poem describing the agonies of Keralites who migrated to work in the tea gardens of Assam.

> To be able to love, to live,
> to hope and also to grieve
> in one's homeland is
> the ultimate bliss .

Alikka's death led me to the mortuary of the Central Hospital, Abu Dhabi. His friends and relatives were assembled there, including Avran, Alikka's brother in law. For years now they were not on talking terms. The body was being given a bath. My ears caught snippets of conversation.

-Last week he came to the Kerala Samajam and talked so enthusiastically…..

-Alikka used to snore loudly. When roommates complained he moved to the mosque or courtyard.

-About life's struggle he would say – they come in waves one after another, never ending

138

Whispers continued. It was time to lower the body into the coffin. Before closing the lid, the customary announcement came : *last chance to glance at the diseased.*

I moved away, I couldn't bear to look at Alikka's lifeless face. ....Floodgates of grief flung open, my heart suppressed a sob.

Here ends the journey of one's Loves, dreams and hopes like footprints erased by the desert

(Ghazi Al Gosaibi)

Someone came forward and placed a floral wreath on the coffin. "No, No. This is un-Islamic," Arab Imam had the wreath removed.

So many kilograms of cargo. That is how dead bodies are airlifted. Alikka too would go home worth his weight. There a group of people wearing white would carry him to the burial ground chanting - *la ilahi illallahi......*

Months later, when I went to Kerala, I visited Alikka's family. His photo on the doorway smiled at

139

me. Old dilapidated house, soiled walls….. I met Alikka's widow- clad in white she reminded me of a da Vinci painting; autumn hadn't yet knocked at her door yet….　■

Here we all believe in tears
One drop for farewell, two for welcome

(Ghazi Al Gosaibi)

THE LEGACY OF OMEIR BIN YOUSUF

One

Benevolence
of the desert

In the heart of Abu Dhabi city, between the Hamdan and Electra streets dwarfed among the high risers stand a few blocks, just 5 storey high. When these were brand new and about to be allotted to prospective owners, the Iraq- Kuwait war broke out. In a swift move UAE authorities converted these flats into government guest houses for refugees fleeing from the uncertainties of Kuwait. Groups of men, women and children impatiently waited in these transit accommodations

for the conflict to be over; so did their mud splashed jeeps and land rovers in the parking lot below.

When the conflict was over, refugees returned to their nests and UAE Government threw open the flats for foreigners. Standing patiently in the queue for several hours, I too got a flat allotted in my name. Thus my family and me stayed there for the next few years listening to the pulse of the city. My office too was close by. But more important, we were in the vicinity of the cherished heritage of Omeir Bin Yousef: his date palms, his Mosque and his Travel Agency .

A large square courtyard. Each side bounded by blocks of 5 story buildings. Lower level houses shopping arcade and restaurants. In the centre of the tiled courtyard stand a pair of aged, decrepit palm trees forgotten by time. These are the palm trees of Omeir Bin Yousuf, I am told.

Rising up to a height of almost 4 meters, the twin trees, a male female pair I guess, never escape my eyes. Like Omeir, his trees too are yellow with age. Perhaps they are yearning for care and nurture or silently suffering the neglect and loneliness. Or perhaps they are reminiscing the good old days of youth and health. Their leaves are brown, even fresh shoots have an ashen shade. The female tree carries an emaciated bunch of fruits as if telling me *"I haven't forgotten my obligation; I am destined to pass on the kindness and compassion of the desert to you, son."* I pick up a fallen fruit and nibble, very sweet.

Omeir Bin Yousuf too is an old man. With flowing white beard and wrinkled oval face, he reminds me of Santa Claus. Every day morning and evening he arrives in his high end luxury car and spends time at the square. Shading his eyes with his palm he glances up at the trees and complains to his driver : "Look, Abdullah, the leaves have wilted; Mushtaq Ali is not watering them daily" All the waste water from Chittangong restaurant should reach the roots of the twin palms- that is Omeir's order to Mushtaq Ali.

Exasperated, driver Abdulla goes in search of Mushataq Ali, the owner of Chittagong restaurant in the square. Mushtaq Ali arrives, in all humility bows and salutes and vigorously defends himself, in Arabic with a heavy Bengali accent. Appropriate body language would reinforces his statements. Omeir listens and nods " Sein, sein" Alright, alright......

How old are trees ? How many generations would they have seen? I enquired around, but couldn't get a precise answer. Almost all said " ever since I can remember...". Omeir , I am sure would have several nostalgic stories to share. Not so long ago on this very piece of land stood Omeir's old ancestral house and the twin trees adorned the courtyard. Omeir's forefathers had migrated from Iran to the Gulf cost to dive for pearls. The sweetness of the fruits might have to a great measure consoled and comforted those earlier generations against the intensity of blazing winds, sandstorms and freezing cold. Family members would have gathered under the shade of these trees; the leaves would have been green and young then; mothers would have passed on folklores, tales of djins and devils to children … stories about the djin who arrives in disguise during hot blazing afternoons and tempts kids: the one who feeds on my left breast is my dearest….. Those days these palm trees must have been young and elegant…..

Palm trees! They set the pace and pattern of community life in the desert. During pollination time female trees bring forth bunches of flowers and male trees burst with sheaths full of pollen. The flowers are then hand pollinated with fresh pollen. In two or three months fruits begin to bud and slowly mature into heavy yellow bunches…. Time to provide props…. Female trees need support to carry the heavy load….

It is celebration time too... Men, women and children gather under the trees... Women ululate and sing... Fatima would have poured out the anxieties of the whole community into her melodious songs......*impending harvest and young unmarried daughters....*

Delicious fruits that ripen untimely
Rob me of my sleep certainly
And alas! lead my mind astray

Imam Ali too would have stopped by in one of his nomadic tours... Putting down his bundle under the tree, sipping suleimani, he would have entertained the villagers with fantasy tales... in return they would have rewarded him with small coins and fresh and hot *luqaimats* .

Those cock and bull stories I spun
Weren't they delightful and fun?
Now who will run
And fetch me a freshly fried luqaimat bun?

Except for the twin haggard palm trees, this city hasn't retained any trace of the olden days. When the old nondescript fishing village morphed into a concrete jungle of wide boulevards and shopping arcades, local

Arabs withdrew to the suburbs. There they settled in red roofed modern villas complete with latest amenities. Today the luxurious suburbs rival the grandeur of the city itself. For the sake of tourists, the Culture Department has showcased the past in the *Heritage Village*. The last of the old generation who are nostalgic can also relive the past there, momentarily...

It was during hectic days of the urbanization and expansion of the city that Omeir surrendered his ancestral property and moved to Al Batein locality. The severance must have been agonizing. To leave these premises: the house where his family lived for generations, the soothing shade of the twin palm trees, the mosque nearby where the family prayed 5 times a day.... Omeir couldn't snap the bond with past so easily. Hence with driver Abdulla at the wheel his luxury car rolls into the square every day, morning and evening. Omeir caresses the twin trees, visits the mosque, and spends time with his childhood friend Hussain Ahmed, who runs a small shop which sells akaal, kefiyeh and traditional footwear.... I would often see driver Abdulla waiting outside the shop *"Arbabab is inside"* he would whisper....

While handing over the ancestral land in the city centre to the authorities to build five storey buildings, Omeir put forward one condition: the twin palms must be preserved at all costs. He also renovated the mosque at his own expense.

Omeir is very rich, owns an empire of business establishments. Travel agency, dealership of General Motors, several skyscrapers, luxury villas in most of the European cities...... His eldest son was the minister for Oil & Gas in the previous government. Having handed over the reins of the business empire to his sons Omeir now wants to enjoy his sunset days....

Omeir is unassuming and simple. He joins the queue in the bank, waiting for his turn. Alarmed, bank manager rushes to him with instant service .. Omeir mumbles.. " *Malish..malish..* don't worry.... " . He goes to fish market and bargains for Sheri and Hamoor, pokes the fish and pries open its gills to check for freshness .. when the deal is done, he lifts the bag, tells the driver *"My hands are dirty and smelly.. let us not dirty the car... you go."* He walks patiently waiting for traffic lights to turn green......

149

Driver Abdulla fills me with stories of his Arbab's philanthropic deeds… generous contributions to *yateemkhanas* world over…

Here Sun doesn't blink;
moon not cradled in clouds
Nor dawn shrouded in mist

Here life is an innocent belle unsullied
by cunning and deceit

Here all believe in tears;
one drop for farewell and two for reunion

(Ghazi Al Gosaibi)

Sitting inside the cool comfort of the air-conditioned room I wonder: Where is the desert? Where are its springs of kindness and compassion?

Omeir glides into my thoughts, so does the withered palm trees …. I can see the link…..

Two

As seasons come and go

Windows open wide to reveal nature's green canvas. Streaks of sunlight playing on coconut palms, banana plants, jackfruit trees blushing and willowing in the breeze. Hiding in the green bush a cuckoo sings sweetly. Swarms of colorful butterflies during day time and twinkling fireflies during night adorn the bushes. Unending ,lazy winding dirt roads like a python. On both sides of the dirt road trees with thick foliage: a canopy as mysterious as a puzzle... And the music of the night rain ...

Watching the videos that I had captured during a recent visit to Kerala, my Yemeni friend Mohsin who comes from the Hadhramaut mountains remarks: The wild beauty of your country overwhelms me. My birthplace, Aden was once upon a time a crater. I will carry the music of these greeneries close to my heart against the fiery winds of the desert....

Morning. Chirpy birds try to wake my child: *it is time to get up and get ready for school.* His sleepy eyes widen ever so slowly with innocent curiosity as he notices, beyond the glass windows, a row of sparrows fidgeting on the balcony railing....

Through the plate glass windows I can see an evergreen eucalyptus tree. Intertwined with its trunk stands a ghaf tree with tiny green foliage. Sparrows have made them their abode. During winter months, when air-conditioners fall silent, we wake up to the twitter of the birds, to a sense of nostalgia.

The old grocery shop in the neighborhood raises its shutters at seven in the morning. Its owner, Sindhi merchant Chabildas Bhojraj is a ripe old man. Bent with age, he walks with difficulty, squeezes his eyes to see better. Still, he arrives every day morning in his son's Imapla car. Then holding a bowl of grain he walks to the eucalyptus tree; glances up at the foliage and claps. Sparrows descend, fill their stomach and fly off, next come a flock of pigeons.....

Inside the shop, he sits and carefully counts coins, holding each coin close to his eyes hooded by thick white eyebrows... Behind him on the wall hangs an old black and white photograph- Sheikh Zaid embracing Bhojraj . That history goes back to more than half a century. ....

More than fifty years ago Abu Dhabi was a tiny fishing hamlet. Population about two thousand, they depended on fishing and pearl diving for livelihood. Camels and donkeys brought water from far away sources. Caravans provided the only link with the outside world. Their chieftain's palace with a canon in regal display was nearby. Chabildas imported goods from Bombay coast and stored in his warehouse in the Abu Dhabi market. He sold for cash and credit. His shop was the nerve centre of Abu Dhabi. Today in the westernized city, Chabildas is irrelevant, like the old faded black and white photograph.

Days go by. The very same repetitive routine. Sparrows and pigeons do their best to alleviate the monotony of our lives.

Summer. Blazing winds coax date fruits to ripen and turn dark. Sparrows take refuge in our balcony. They perch on the railings. *Look they are thirsty,* I guide my son to the balcony with a mug full of water. Birds fidget and dirty the balcony. Later I hear my wife's exasperation as she cleans the railings .....

Sweltering days. Sea breeze dense with moisture. In the continuous growling of the air conditioners, city sounds get drowned. Moisture condenses on the glass panes and masks city sights. Venture out and you feel unquenchable thirst....

Rain. A providential blessing. Just a splatter, yet rare and precious. Rarer still, the luxury of a downpour with the accompaniments of lightning and thunder. Al Gosaibi's lines come to my mind

Rain !Torrential rain !
Like the endless tears of a woman
Weeping over her lost love.

We barge into the balcony to welcome the desert rain, listen for the twitter and flutter of birds nesting in the nearby trees and recite Sayyab's Rain Song. " from every rain drop blooms yellow and red blossoms."

The sorrows that rain can prompt,
The sobs of gutters when it pours,
How lost a loner feels

Nostalgia for monsoon is rekindled. As the rainwater gushes through the broken drains do I also hear the suppressed sobs of lonely migrant workers?

Winter. Dry and cold. Roaring winds shake the big trees sheltered among skyscrapers. Then come the icy winds originating from far away glaciers. We snuggle into the warmth of woolens. Wrapped in warm clothes, junior has just returned from school. Mother tells him affectionately "Don't go out; this cold weather is not good for you."

But Khader? Arms folded across his chest he walks around in half sleeves shirt. He is the delivery boy of the nearby supermarket. *Aren't you feeling cold?*

I enquire. With a smile he dissolves into the roaring wind.

Dust storms: For days sun remains hidden behind a dust curtain. Wind furiously sweeps up the dust and garbage into a twirl and deposits in our balconies. From behind the safety of closed windows, we watch the branches of eucalyptus and ghaf trees swaying wildly.

City stands bathed in the brilliance of neon and sodium lamps. Vehicles whizz past. Mammoth cranes capable of rotating a full circle are busy day and night. New high risers are being built. We have had enough of all this. Fed up with the concrete jungle, we yearn for our village, its sights and sounds. Rural settings, starlit skies and chirping crickets... This city has nothing new to offer; its sights have lost their novelty. Corniche sunsets, tourist dhows, rows of palm trees- we are bored with all that. We withdraw to the confines of our flat. Withered palm trees in the courtyard remind me of my decrepit parents . Lonely and helpless they are awaiting my return. During my intermittent visits, father pleads: *Son, this house is yours, you designed it, you built with your hard earned money; you chose the furniture*

,furnishings, decorations…. When would you come and enjoy all these?

Suppressed sobs leave the sentence incomplete.

Friday evenings. Telephone line becomes the umbilical chord transfusing maternal warmth. Mother's sleepy feeble voice *"Son, you left home in a cold November. It has been decades since…."*

Yes, I do remember. Decades ago a cold November ….crossing the Arabian sea in a cargo boat …. the rumor of my death… a mother's agony and grief …

Days lengthen into weeks, months and years… The evergreen eucalyptus outside my window stands still as if frozen in the flight path of time… Or is it Time that has frozen?

Three

The Friday Crowd

Fridays. As the day progresses, city is inundated with people, a motley crowd of weather beaten faces, world-weary countanances. Bangladeshis with red lips and stained teeth; pashtuns wearing long loose garments and headgear; sardarjis and Pakistani Punjabis with strong smell of mustard oil; thin, emaciated men from Andhra, Tamilnadu and Kerala…. They talk aloud gesticulating and shaking their heads; the buzz fills the air.

They are all from the Indian subcontinent. Having crossed the geopolitical boundaries, they are bound by an unusual sense of solidarity. The other day I along with several others had to wait for a very long time for a taxi. Nothing unusual- at times taxis are aplenty and at other times passengers are aplenty. Ignoring others in the line a taxi came and halted just in front of me. The driver, a Pakistani Pathan cheerfully asked me to get in. Then he said " Did you notice the others? One is Sudanese, the other a Palestinian. I prefer our people."

Hum log that is what he said *Our people*. "See, though we are divided, we share the same roots…" He went on and on.. I felt indeed happy.

When native Arabs moved to posh suburban villas, foreigners occupied the city. On holidays, the city is suddenly and temporarily taken over by poor migrant laborers. They swarm in from I don't know where and

aggregate selectively in different spots. In the square underneath Omeir's palms, people from Indian subcontinent throng; behind the Jawasat Road next to the Sudan Club, East Africans unite: Yemenis Somalians, Sudanese.;. next to the Gas station in the souk shabbily dressed Egyptians assemble ; in the vicinity of the Saab Municipal building Syrians and Palestinians meet...

Where does this diverse crowd come from? I am curious. Rows and rows of buses parked under the Eti Salat building gave the answer. These are construction workers housed in makeshift labor camps beyond the Maqta bridge. Friday is their day of leisure and rest. Their employers are kind enough to provide transportation. They come to the city for shopping and recreation or just to get away from the barrenness of the desert.

City shops wait for the Friday crowd. Friday business compensates for the dull week days. There are at least ten restaurants in the square : Chittangong Restaurant by Bangladeshi Mushtaq Ali, Jaffer Restaurant by a Karachiwala, Taha cool Bar by Keralie Mammadkka , ... the list is long. Regional specialities

159

like gulab Jamun, rasgolla, jilebi, over sized samosas; parippu vada, pazhampori, sukhian... you name it . Kerala Saloon and Karachi Hair Cutting Shop are crowded on Fridays . The Alam supermarket also does good business. But unlike the urbane middle class customers the Friday crowd doesn't care for a shopping basket or trolley. They hold their goods in hand or close to their chest.... impatient, they push the line if there is a delay....

Sitting under Omeir's palm trees, many share their sorrows and traumas. I snatch bits and pieces of conversations as I walk by-

—No wages for 6 months now.. forgot when I last remitted money home...Company has to get a huge cheque from somewhere I believe....

-My visa will expire soon. They demand five thousand for renewal....

-Mother is sick, should go and see her at the earliest. But how? Leave, money... ticket..... how can I manage all these in a short time....

Mostly distress and frustrations. There are terrifying experiences too

-Last week a tourist couple gave me their camera and asked me to take a few photographs of them... I clicked... Nothing unusual that is what I thought... But soon a group of policemen pounced on me and took me to the police station. Then the questioning started: who were they? Which buildings were photographed? How much they paid me? A barrage of questions... I was flabbergasted. It seems the photographs were taken in a no camera zone front of an embassy. The police detained me for four days..... the trauma I went through......

Mrs George who lives in the upper level, is agitated for another reason. *It is impossible to go out on Friday evenings...* I understand. My family too avoids going out on Friday evenings. The lustful, scorching eyes have the power to disrobe a female, any female; the experience could be unnerving. Mrs George suggests that we write about this in Khaleej Times, or complain to authorities. The other day a Bengali youth joined her in the lift, *just for fun* he said. He was getting uncomfortably closer... terrified she fled back to safety of her flat.

Taha Cool Bar is famous for its tasty food. Mammdkka does brisk business, I tease him *so you own the whole of your village now?* Mammadkka rubs his graying beard and grins *Oh no no, I have debts to repay.... Even yesterday I had to plead with Sardarji...*

I am shocked! Sardarji is the notorious loan shark in town. He extracts daily interest. He first grabs the victim's passport, collects post dated checks; then deducts the first installment of interest and then advances the loan. The victim can't escape. Despite stringent laws of the land, moneylenders flourish. They hover around hawk-eyed implementing their own parallel laws.

Khader the delivery boy of Saji Groceries, sweeps past me like a shadow. When he joined the job, he was a healthy youngster. Now he is thin and emaciated. Up and down the stairs he flies, delivering items ordered over the phone by the occupants of the high-riser apartment complexes. Hot afternoons and sweltering evenings and wintry nights- he appears and disappears with the quickness of a phantom. What is he worried about, what are his sorrows? ... *paltry wages, visa which would expire soon*, he replies. His dreams are minimal a good salary and a proper visa.

Looking down through my glass window, I see life flowing by, I try to feel its pulse. Below, at ground level I notice the crowd in Abdul Khayam Trours & Travels. Visa rules are being tightened. Illegal migrant workers must go back home. Government has announced a grace period of just one month. Khayyam Travel Agency has scheduled daily chartered flights to Dhakka ; even that is not enough to meet the demand….. Yesterday there was an unending line of Bangladeshis clamoring for tickets to go home.

Shop owners are a happy lot. Because the homebound migrants are busy shopping. In small groups they enter each shop, bargain and buy. A Pashtun's dreams are limited to woolen blankets and tape recorders. Tall and handsome, his chiseled features are shrouded by the disheveled hair and shabby clothes. He sits in the lonely corners of the public parks and records tapes for his family. Postal department ensures the tape parcels reach the addressee in the frontier villages and brings back replies in the same way. Technology helps the illiterate migrant worker to overcome his shortcomings in a more personalized way. He gets worried when he receives news that tribal rivalries have led to blood shedding in the villages. He plans to earn enough- to buy an AK 47 from the

Peshawar Market, to build a safe, secret basement in his home....

Evening stretches into dark night. City lights come up. Is the city feeling uncomfortable under the glare of neon and sodium lamps? My wife is in no mood to cook dinner; she says let us get Khubz. My daughter prefers Shawarma sandwich. I walk down the stairs to pick up food....

Friday crowd has dispersed leaving the surroundings littered with crushed plastic tea cups, cigarette butts, cola cans and red stains of *paan* on the cement tiles .... Municipal sweepers will arrive before sunrise and tidy up the entire place. A brand new dawn will arrive with no recollection of the previous day's brouhaha. Omeir's palms will sway gently in the dewy morning breeze to live through another day.......

Yet another day. Life's eternal cycle goes on....the drudgery goes on...... ■

Epilogue

Khor Fakkan Calling

To me visiting Khor Fakkan was like "homecoming". Not only because it was my first touch down point in the Persian Gulf, but also because it had crows. Nowhere else in the Gulf you can find crows. For the people in the Indian subcontinent, crows are an integral part of daily life, representing the most mundane and the most sublime. About crows there are nursery rhymes and philosophical poems. According to the Hindu belief, crows are the proxy for departed souls. There is even a solemn annual ritual of feeding crows in memory of ancestors....

Sunil who has made an odyssey into the historical alleys of Khor Fakkan claims crows would have migrated from Ran of Kutch to Khor Fakkan. Perhaps in one of the boats. Then they made this shore their home settled and multiplied. Maybe . But these birds stir up a sense of loss in me. I realize how much I miss my village, my home, its surrounding greenery, old fashioned well, pond and above all my mother. Prasad

comments : look, these are Arab crows. But I am in no mood to listen. I pour my heart out to the birds- that I am fed up with the city life, that I feel suffocated inside the concrete towers, that frozen meat and fish have wreaked havoc on my taste buds, that artificial city lights have estranged the moon and the stars , that I am disgusted with the make believe world thrown open before me by the home theaters and TV channels.......

Then I declare aloud voice : That for a change I always return to the crows of Khor Fakkan.

A series of holidays. As time hangs heavy in my hands I immerse myself in Tawfiq Sayigh *And then?* That is when Prasad's voice floats over the phone- *Come, come to Khor Fakkan...*

Shorter days and long cooler nights of autumn. Ideal for a vacation, a brief escape from the bustling city life. We take the highway from Abu Dhabi touching upon Dubai, Sharjah and Dhaid en route. The landscape changes continuously- typical desert scenes with camels and palm trees; modern architectural wonders; green-houses enclosing vegetable gardens;

oil fields with burning pits; signboards of KFC, Mc Donald, cola. Just like the desert highways in California, my friend said.

The highway is crowded. European and American vehicles whiz past us. They are heading to the beach with colorful umbrellas and ice boxes stacked with chilled beer cans. Seawater and sun will work together on their skin and temper it to a reddish tan. Then for about a week they will proudly show off their tan in memory of the just concluded beach vacation.

We reach Dhaid. Far away we can see thick blue ridges like earth's varicose veins. Those are Khor Fakkan ranges extending to the Hajar mountains. Will there be elephants, tigers and lions? My little daughter is curious. I comfort her- no, at the most mountain foxes and wild cats. Those are dry rocks with thistles and thorns....

Then we visit wadis, dried river beds. Once upon a time these might have been mighty rivers, with thick forests on both sides where dinosaurs during prehistoric times and much later lions and tigers might have freely roamed... I tell my daughter. Some wadis have an abundance of sub-surface water. Rainfall recharges these sub surface reservoirs. Before the era of desalination plants, groundwater abstracted from these aquifers was the only source of fresh water for domestic use in northern emirates.

Geological surveys have established that Hajar mountains are mostly limestone. That has led to mushrooming of cement factories in the vicinity. In summer limestones get roasted, radiate heat and stir up hot fiery winds. At such times Prasad's voice would float over the phone " Living in an inferno….."

Decades ago, in a cold November, I had ascended and descended the slopes of those rough mountain ranges- that memory has been relegated to the distant past. That uneven rocky mountain path has been evened out into a satin smooth two lane highway. This is not the handiwork of the old man of the legends, but the power of petrodollars.

The rough mountain ranges and ridges always stood as impregnable fortifications safeguarding tribal territories. During the seventh century these ranges protected the Ibadi territory of Oman when it dared to break away from Khalifa, Tribes lived in geological isolation in inaccessible interiors with no contact with the outside world. Prasad said -Even now there are such tribes, living practically in the stone age. Sensing my curiosity, he despairs: *If only Rajan were with us! Rajan could have given you more information. But alas!*

Rajan Iyer from Palakkad was with the Geological Survey of the Emirates. He knew these ranges like the back of his hand. Colleagues and superiors alike praised him for his commitment and capability. Once during an official survey, his vehicle toppled over the ranges and the gorge below swallowed him. Condolences poured in, columns were written about him in local newspapers. ....

As we move on I spot a Bedouin on the roadside with an array of bottles in front of him. Wild honey !. Supermarkets are flooded with various brands of purified honey in attractive packages. But I am tempted for the unrefined, natural stuff. We stop the car. He says *"thimanian dirham"* eighty dirhams for this stuff, I am shocked. He is confident of his product: *Number wahat*, super grade. He opens a bottle, dips his right index finger inside , pulls it out and asks me to taste.

Disgusted and outraged at his barbaric ways I rush back to the car.

As the vehicle rolls forward, satin smooth road becomes rough and uneven.- we are cruising along the border between Oman and UAE. Oman has a small territory landlocked within UAE mountains. Often Khor Fakkan tribes clash with Oman tribes. Both sides believe in blood for blood and life for life.

When troops of the foe are far,
Our javelins we dart
And when we close in combat
We strike with sabres sharp
Slender and dark our javelins
made from delicate reeds of Kathaian.
We cleave enemies in pieces
Cut down their necks with sickles.
We lead on our troop
like a mountain with a pointed summit
We preserve our reputation
And advance in foremost ranks
With youth who consider death as completion of glory
And with aged heroes experienced in war

(Amru bin Kulthoom: Golden Odes)

At times the warring tribes descend into the highway like a swarm of bees and hold up traffic for hours or for days. Then military trucks would arrive and take control of the situation. After peaking for a while, everything subsides, enemies withdraw to their respective mountain habitats. Khor Fakkan ranges stand mute witness to what man does to man.

We reach Khor Fakkan. It is no longer the crumbling medieval fishing hamlet. It has transformed itself into a port city. A Holiday Inn Hotel on the beach. Rocks jut out to the sea. Fishing boats, dhows, sea gulls and ships anchored in the outer sea. Beyond that lies the Indian ocean. Sea breeze whizzes past us ......with it we glide into the past...

Weather beaten cargo boats carrying a load of humans. The passengers had embarked on this voyage with high hopes. As the the turbulent sea shook the boat violently they prayed to gods and prophets alike...

Chandramohan recounted his experiences: " *Noaha's arc. That is what we called our boat. After weeks at sea we reached the shores of Khor Fakkan. We were as good as dead. Starvation and nausea had reduced us to skeletons. For days we hadn't had a bath. With matted hair and vacant eyes, as I walked on the beach, a group of Arab children playing there saw me, they shouted and laughed. When they started hurling stones at me, I ran. The beach trail ended among the rocks jutting out into the sea, I took refuge there. I could hear nothing but the rumblings of the sea and the roaring of the wind. Nearby was a garbage dump and crows were pecking at it. I sat like a stone, numb, unfeeling.*

I got help from several people during my stay in Khor Fakkan. Having starved for extended periods, I was ever hungry and greedy for food. It took days to get over that and eat in peace. I did odd jobs. My first job was in a brick kiln, to drive away crows which might otherwise shit on the freshly baked bricks. There were no toilet facilities we relieved ourselves on the beach. Migrants and poor Arabs sat in rows. So did women and children . Some men were sea farers others were engaged in roadwork. An East-West highway was being built extending all the way to Khor Fakkan. Many of the newly arrived migrants joined the road work as unskilled labourers. They bore into the rocks to make tunnels and built bridges over gorges. Some worked as time keepers…. Everyday early morning, company vehicle would arrive to pick us up and transport to the work site; in the evening we would be brought back to Khor Fakkan. The only entertainment was Hindi films shown in an open air theatre. TV hadn't arrived . Babu was one among us. He was my neighbour back at home. His ways were strange, often giving in to sudden impulses. He worked for two months as a labourer. Then with the earnings he bought a set of western clothes from a second-hands shop and moved to Dubai. He dreamt of living like a "sahib". Later we heard that he was back in Kerala, then that he was in a mental asylum and finally that he committed suicide…….

Several migrant labourers perished in the sea ; perhaps an equal number perished on the land too. Their stories remain untold…..

Prasad's house- the gate opens to a small front-yard. Beyond that a cute house . Two bedrooms, kitchen, sitting room . A compound wall about 6 feet high protects the property. From the front yard one can see the blue ridges of Khor Fakkan mountain. But that is not what catches my attention; I am bowled over by the drumstick tree in full bloom in one corner of the front yard. My taste buds crave for the ethnic delicacies- with the leaves, with the flowers and of course with the drumsticks......

I thoroughly enjoy the house and its rural setting. Sun goes down splashing colours over the sky, and stars begin to twinkle . As moon rises from behind the ranges, the valleys are bathed in moonlight and the mountain peaks appear darker. Cities and deserts are forgotten, trials and tribulations of professional life are forgotten, limits and limitations of the migrant life are forgotten..... As a misty chill wraps around me I feel serene......

Then the barbecue party begins. A rather big group of family and friends. Jawahar works in the Supermarket owned by an Arab, Pushpan is a salesman for a Japanese showroom , Prasad and I with our families. It is strory time. We touch upon everything

- pranks during college days, petty quarrels, monsoon, slushy, slippery embankments, harvest time.... we relive the past with cold bear and grilled meat. It continues till late in the night. We could hear a troop of mountain foxes howling in chorus. I notice fear lurking in my daughter's eyes. Finally we retire to sleep.

Cold descends from the Khor Fakkan ranges. Snug in warm blankets we slip into sleep.

Roosters in the neighbourhood announce the arrival of dawn. Crows too have woken up. Prasad is taking us to nearby farms. By the time we reach the farm it is hot. Cucumbers, green and yellow lemon, banana plants heavy with the tiered bunches, mango trees in full bloom.... among them we spot a few saplings of tapioca... *Must be some the handiwork of a Malayali*, Prasad chuckles....

We bargain with the farmer for bananas. Old man is not sure of the price. He calls Amna, his not so old wife. *Thneen dirham* she says. Two dirham? We agree. As the old man axes the plant., it falls with a screech.

A basketful of tapioca has also been dug up for us. But there is no weighing balance. We agree on a lump sum price…. What about mangoes? But they are very costly, we say *no, thank you.*

We could hear water gushing out of tube well and filling a tank. From the tank, through a network of channels the entire farm is irrigated. With the farmer's permission, we jump into the huge tank- Fresh and cool water… such a refreshing feeling. Like jumping into the village pond back at home…

We drive through the mountain roads. Village farmers have set up roadside shops to sell their produce. In these fertile green valleys where tomato, tapioca , pomegranate, water melon and cucumber flourish we wander with a sense of loss, not quite sure what exactly did we lose…

Evening. Time to return to Abu Dhabi. Fresh vegetables and fruits are stuffed in the trunk/ Those are for friends….My wife plucks bunches of leaves from the drumstick tree. The tree smiles bestowing tiny white flowers on us……

Many more such Khor Fakkan visits….. The trip with Chandrashekharan and Janardhandas. One created artwork with fingers and the other with camera. Once we videographed a herd of camels grazing lazily. Unmindful of us the herd went on with their business of champing and chewing for a very long time. Usually they are calm and quiet but if aroused could kick you with forelegs and crunch your bones with teeth. Male camels are more dangerous especially when in heat. I was trying to recollect passages from Thesiger's *The sands of Arabia* , when one of the camels lunged forward. We panicked and almost ran for life. Then from a safe distance we laughed at ourselves.

Our four wheel drive rolled over the uneven mountain path. No trace of flora or fauna anywhere. Just tire marks of earlier vehicles. Sunil had full knowledge of the geography of Khor Fakkan. We were in search of the much famed waterfalls tucked away somewhere in the mountain ranges. We weren't sure of the path, at times we thought we were lost. The day was getting hotter by the minute. Then slowly we could see the mist in the air and hear a faint sound of water fall. When we finally reached the spot, it was indeed a disappointment- a thin stream rolling down the boulders high up and forming a small pool below. I had seen mightier waterfalls elsewhere. But a natural fresh water stream in the middle of the desert – that made all the difference. Earlier visitors had defaced the surrounding rocks with scrawls in Arabic . We jumped into the waist high water in the pool, then climbed over the rocks in search of the source of waterfall. Trekking along the water flow, wading through thick wild grass, we moved forward. Cool air refreshed us and jokes gladdened our hearts.

And then we visited the ruins of the old fort and its ramparts and the centuries old mosque made of clay and mud. We took a dip in the hot water springs of Ras al Khaimah. Janardhanadas continuously clicked pictures of landscapes, Bedouins and palm trees. Finally we reached the shores of Khor Fakkan. Lashing onto the rocks, the sea was roaring. Waves collapsed and frothed along the beach. At Khor Fakkan the sea is safe, no hidden currents, nor sharks. Westerners and their irlfriends in scanty beachwear were alternating between the sea and the shore. Janardhandas, who

181

claimed to be a skilful swimmer jumped onto the crust of a breaker and glided into the sea. Wading in shallow waters, we watched him wide eyed. Later, ravenously hungry after the watersports, we consumed all the sandwiches in the restaurant.

During another trip Prasad arranged for us to met Abdulla of the mountain. Like the old man in the Kurosawa film *Dreams*, Abdulla too preferred to stay away from modern technological contraptions; he too didn't approve of mixing up day and night. Abdulla is

worried that during the last two to three decades Bedouin lifestyle has changed considerably with the result that life has lost its spontaneity and purity. He finds it difficult to adapt to the changes. He feels that younger generation might find it easier. Abdulla and family live in a thatched hut made of braided palm leaves. He doesn't have fridge or television. Fridge is not good for health Abdulla said. *"Thatched hut can resist solar heat to a great extent. Mountain breeze will do the rest.* As a part of welfare schemes Government has built flats for them. But Abdulla doesn't want to go there. Earlier we had visited those double level flats. For Bedouins, cattle is *family*, so the animals too go upstairs, one room was set aside for them. The whole place was stinking of dung and urine.

Abdulla gets a pension from the government. He goes to the bank to collect it. That is how Prasad knew him and arranged for our visit. We bought watermelons, oranges and grapes from Fujeira market. In his thatched hut on top of a hillock Abdulla was waiting for us. Age had wrinkled his face. To our greetings he responded with *Aslam Alaikkum*. We presented him with the fruits and sat down on the faded carpets. We were served suleimani tea flavoured with cardom and later quahwah. Plateful of fruits were spread before us. Abdulla's middle aged wife in burqua and little daughter Amina playing with her lamb stood around as curious onlookers. For Abdulla life has not been easy. He has been a toiler at the sea as well as on the land. Dhows took him to Saudi Arabia and Bahrain. He has travelled with caravans on camels and donkeys. All that have been replaced now by Toyota pickups. True, he refused the villa offered by the government but has accepted the vegetable farm.

Amina's lambs jumped and played around. My daughter 's camera captured those moments. Then we paid a visit to Abdullah's farm. There an emaciated man with sunken eyes and stained teeth gave us a feeble smile - an unskilled migrant worker from Bengal. As we bid goodbye to Abdullah and his family, we noticed a Bedouin riding past on a donkey. The animal's stony face in contrast to the rider's dreamy grin amused us to no end. Another snapshot from the past...

Not everything is hunky-dory about Khor Fakkan. It stirs up painful memories too. Like when Prasad's agitated voice came over the phone- "Our friend Jawahar is no more". I couldn't but repeat after him in utter dismay. It wasn't a natural death- either a suicide or a murder.

Of late Jawahar was depressed and withdrawn. He suspected that drug peddlers operated from the warehouse of the supermarket where he worked. The network originated somewhere in the mountains of Afghanistan. Jawahar didn't want to get involved even unknowingly. He was terrified beyond imagination of the consequences of such an eventuality : imprisonment in the infernos of the desert from where there is no escape. He tried to quit his job, but boss wouldn't let him; instead threatened him with dire consequences. With no escape route in sight, he packed off his wife and little son to Kerala. After seeing them off at Sharjah airport he returned to his tiny flat in Khor Fakkan.

Days later close friends with the help of local police broke open the door. They found him dead. Seated in a chair with a noose around his neck. Body had begun to decompose. The usual procedures of

185

law followed- post mortem, mortuary.... When informed, Jawahar's wife vehemently denied the possibility of suicide. Jawahar's family and friends were distraught. They sent Prakasan, a lawyer from their village to Abu Dhabi. We met in my flat. Prakasan wanted to get to the truth. There was pressure from Jawahar's near and dear.

We pondered over the issue at length and came to a conclusion : *Obviously we can't bring back Jawahar. Armed with just a death certificate how far can we go searching for the truth ? It will be just a waste of money and time...*

Much later I heard that Jawahar's widow was eking out a living running an embroidery shop in the coastal city of Kochi . Who would she be blaming for her loss, fate or life itself?,

Since then decades have rolled by. My child who was curious about the mountain lions and tigers has attained youth. Even so passage of time hasn't dimmed the images of Khor Fakkan ranges and valleys . Often my imagination takes wings and transports me to the shores of Khor Fakkan . There I stand clapping for the dear departed souls offering them a fistful of memories in homage.... Crows descend and crowd around me. Among them I search for Jawahar, Rajan, Babu... and thousands more....

Death haunts me forever ; of those who perished in the seas and others who withered on the land.....

■

Footnotes:

1. **Haajiar, Hajji**- A moslem who has undertaken the Hujj pilgrimage.

2..**The Golden Odes**: The *Mu'allaqât* in Arabic. A collection of 7 pre Islamic poems.

3,4,5,6,7 Renowned personalities in Malayalam literature. T.Padmanabhan (shortstories); O.N.V Kurup (Poems); U.A Khader (short stories,novels, travelogues); Ramakrishnan(writer &N translator); Vaikom Muhammad Bashir(Novels & short stories)

8. **Arthur Rimbaud** (1854-1891): French poet who stopped writing at the age of 21

9. Mark 12:7-8

10. **Orde Wingate**(1903-1944) : British Army Officer notorious for ruthlessly crushing Palestine revolt using *Special Night Squads*

11. **Wilfred Thesiger** (1910-2003) : Author of *Arabian Sands*. He crossed the Empty Quarter (Rub' al Khali) twice.

About the Author

Journalist, Writer and Publisher

Born at Engandiyoor, Trichur, Kerala. Left to UAE
in the early seventies. Was a staff of Reuters Bulletin,
the first English newspaper in UAE, based in
Sharjah. Later joined in the Hongkong Bank worked
until 1998 and returned to India. In UAE he was
social worker of Indian Community and mainly
participated in literary and social activities. Served
as a Journalist, wrote columns regularly for
newspapers and magazines about Middle east.
During the Gulf war he worked as a reporter to
Desabhmani. In addition to Dubaipuzha, memoirs
he wrote a novel Katalirampangal (Rumbling seas).
His other works are Marubhoomiyile jalakangal
(The windows of the desert) and Iruttil
Urangathirikkunnu. (Be awaken in the darkness).
Now active in publishing.